Whispers of Mistletoe

Book Two in the Whispers of New England Series

Sue Mills

Choose The Front Row Media

Blurbs

"Quinn Michaels is easing back into dating after briefly reuniting with her high school sweetheart in Whispers of Forgiveness, the prequel to Whispers of Mistletoe. Enter Caden Brady, a tall, dark, and handsome doctor. They live two hours apart, and both have demanding professions and busy lives, but they're drawn to each other like magnets. However, Caden's haunted by the ghost of a traumatic relationship of his own, and he's not sure he will fully trust anyone again. This romantic, steamy book will have readers rooting for Quinn and Caden to find happiness."

Mary M., Line Editor, Red Adept Editing

DEDICATION

To All Who Have Loved and Lost
And Had The Courage To Try Again

Playlist

I'm Shipping Up To Boston – Dropkick Murphys

Enchanted – Taylor Swift (Taylor's Version)

I'll Make Love To You – Boyz II Men

Always Been You – Shawn Mendes

Sure Feels Good – Willie J Healey

Obsessed – Olivia Rodrigo

Biblical – Calum Scott

Fix You – Cold Play

Happier – Ed Sheeran

Labyrinth – Taylor Swift

Contents

Chapter One

Family Dinner

Caden

"Hey, if you've got my number, you know my name. Leave a message, and I'll call you back."

Getting a voicemail greeting rattled Caden Brady's confidence, and he ended the call without saying anything.

Damn, I hoped she'd answer. She responded to my text right away this morning. Maybe she's still on the road.

Caden had met Quinn Michaels the day before at a Healthy Living in the Workplace conference and was instantly captivated. Conversation flowed easily between them, but making the choice to call her was next-level for Caden. He hadn't wanted to talk to a woman in a long time.

He took a deep breath and blew it out as he gazed across Boston Harbor. The weather was mild for early November, and the moon was just peeking above the horizon. Noisy seagulls scuttled along the docks, hoping for a morsel to scavenge. The waterfront teemed with restaurants, hotels, and luxury condominiums. He watched a plane land on the opposite side of the harbor before continuing on his way to their condo for dinner.

When he arrived at their building, Caden pushed the button to let them know he'd arrived. His fingers drummed near the door as he waited.

Come on, Ma. You knew I was coming—answer the damn door. Caden's family had moved to the waterfront from his boyhood home in South Boston several years earlier. He missed being able to let himself in when he arrived, like at the old house. *It'll never be home like Southie was.* The buzzer finally sounded, and when he reached their top-floor condo, he gathered his mother into a hug.

"Hey Ma, dinner smells good."

"We'll eat when your sister arrives. There's beer in the fridge, and Dad's in the living room."

After grabbing a beer, Caden walked into the living room, glancing out the wall of windows overlooking the harbor. Twisting the cap, he sank onto the leather sectional. "Hey, Dad, how's it going?"

"Good, doc, good. It's been too long since we've seen you. How's life at Mass General?"

"Are you stealing Mom's line about how long it's been since you've seen me? The hospital's crazy busy. I've had two doctors, and a nurse transfer out. They didn't like the hectic pace in the Emergency Department."

"You know how it is. Your mother misses you if it goes more than a couple of weeks between visits. But the holidays are coming up, so we'll see you more. And you'll be going up to Hanover when the baby is born, right?"

"I wouldn't miss it." His older sister, Claire, lived two hours north of Boston in New Hampshire, and was expecting a child in a few weeks. "About time we got another boy. I've been carrying the weight for the Bradys for thirty-two years. It's been a burden." He grinned as he stretched his long legs out on the ottoman and took a swallow of his beer. "But someone had to do it."

Chrissy, the youngest of the siblings, came out of her bedroom, and Caden rose to give her a brief hug.

"Long time no see, big brother."

He shook his head. "Is Ma paying everyone to harass me? First Dad and now you."

Chrissy grinned. "You know Mom."

He laughed and put his arm over her shoulder as they walked to the dining room.

Chloe, the third Brady kid, was placing the silverware on the table laden with salmon, rice pilaf, roasted broccoli, and rolls. Caden smiled, thinking about how his mother stuck to the old-school practice of serving fish on Friday. She didn't adhere to much of her Catholic upbringing, but fish on Friday was a tradition still honored even though it was no longer required by the Church.

When they were all seated, Caden watched his mother look around the table, and he knew she was pleased to have all but two of her children there. Claire was in New Hampshire, and his fourth sister, Cathleen, lived in North Carolina.

"Let's do something we did when you were little," Mom said. "Tell us the best thing that happened to you this week."

All three of the kids groaned, but Caden sensed his mother had something to share and was building up to it.

"Humor your mother," Dad said, a shit-eating grin on his face. He pointed at Caden. "You're the oldest. You go first."

Caden narrowed his eyes as he looked at his father. *They're both in on whatever is going on. Quinn. Meeting Quinn was the best thing that happened to me this week, but I am most definitely not sharing that.*

Caden struggled to come up with something else interesting and finally said, "My latest presentation received an A. And I feel like a proud third grader telling you all that." He laughed along with his sisters.

His mother clapped her hands. "How many more credits until you get that master's in hospital administration?"

"I'll be done in the spring."

Chloe groaned. "That's lame! First, getting an A is nothing new for you, and second, that's the best you can—"

"Oh wait! I do have something else," Caden said, interrupting Chloe. "I delivered a baby this afternoon!"

"Show-off!" Chloe groaned. "Well, my news, which looks pathetic beside Cade delivering a baby, is that Tim and I booked a trip to the Bahamas for our February vacation. We're going to escape the Boston winter."

Mom looked excited. "Do you think he's going to propose? And where is he tonight, anyway?"

"Mom! It's just a vacation. Geesh!" Chloe shook her head. "He and the other advisor to the senior class are helping them get ready for homecoming."

Chrissy piped up. "My turn. I submitted my application to Boston University this week."

Caden extended his hand to high-five her. "That's great. Have you added any other schools to the mix? And you're still looking at nursing?" Chrissy was fifteen years younger than him, but he was one of her biggest cheerleaders.

She nodded. "Yes, still nursing. You convinced me it would offer the most opportunities. I'll be finishing the rest of the applications this week for the schools we've talked about. And I've added Norwich in Vermont."

The mention of Vermont brought his thoughts back to Quinn. She'd said she had grown up in northern Vermont. *Jesus, you need to get a grip on yourself about this woman.*

"Okay, Ma, your turn," he said. "You and Dad obviously have something to tell us."

His parents looked at each other, Mom nodding at Dad. "Do you want to tell them? Or shall I?"

"Go ahead. I know how hard it's been for you to keep it quiet."

Her face glowed with a wide smile. "We've bought a house in Florida!"

"Specifically, Fort Myers," Dad added. "We're going to spend part of the winter down there. I can work remotely. Your mom is going to cut back a little. Plus, her buying trips for the store can originate as easily from there as from here. We'll head down there after Christmas."

The kids all congratulated them, and Chloe asked if there would be room for them to visit.

"Of course!" their mom said. "It has four bedrooms, and we want you all to spend time there, with us or without." While they all chattered about the house, she took out her phone to show them pictures.

Caden raised his eyebrows in shock. "Whoa, Ma, is this the apocalypse?" His mother firmly forbade phones at the table.

Her cheeks reddened. "I'm learning to be more flexible."

Everyone rolled their eyes at her.

To change the subject, she asked Caden about Thanksgiving. "Do you have to work?"

Caden absorbed her pointed look. Every year, it was the same thing. He tried not to sound too exasperated when he said, "I work every Thanksgiving so people with families can enjoy the holiday together."

His mom frowned. "You have a family."

Chloe and Chrissy looked on in silence. The discussion was not new.

"Yes, I do. You know I'm talking about families with small children." He put his fork down and stared at his mother. Caden, even more than his sisters, shared her strong will. "My shift will end at three. You can have a nice leisurely day to cook the feast. No getting up at the crack of dawn to put the turkey in."

"Next year, there will be a little one," she reminded him. "Claire and James will have their baby boy."

"And I'll take that into consideration next year, but this year, I'm working."

Mom sighed and went to the kitchen to get the cake she had baked for dessert. As she placed a slice on his plate, she asked, "Cade, do you remember Jane Murphy from the neighborhood?"

Uh-oh. This required caution. "Yes," he intoned. "Why?"

"Her mother and I had coffee this week, and Jane's moving back to Boston. She's been in New Jersey since she finished college."

"Well, good for her. Boston's got it all going on over Jersey."

"I could get her number for you. Her mother said she just left a long-term relationship."

His jaw tightened. "No, Ma. No."

"But…"

He put his hand up. "Between work and classes, I don't have extra time to take someone out to dinner or anything else."

The girls grinned at each other. He knew they were happy their mother was bugging him, which got them off the hook for once, but he shot them a *help me* look.

Thankfully, Chrissy spoke up. "Come on, Mom, don't push him. Maybe he's exploring his sexual orientation and isn't ready to share with us."

Chloe and his father burst into laughter as Caden groaned and looked to the ceiling, muttering, "Oh my God."

Chrissy shrugged and grinned at him as she dug into her piece of cake.

To Caden's great relief, it seemed Chrissy's comment shut down the conversation about him calling Jane Murphy. The last thing he needed was his mother getting involved in his dating life.

After they all helped clear the table, Caden hugged his mother. "I'm going to head out. I won't let it go so long before I stop by again, I promise." He looked at Chrissy with his eyes twinkling. "I'll get you back, squirt."

Caden and Chloe left together, and when they got to the sidewalk, a mild breeze coming off the ocean ruffled his hair. The moon hung overhead, shining on the streets.

Caden glanced at his sister. "I'm going to walk home. What about you?"

"I've called an Uber."

He waited with her, chatting easily, until the car arrived. He opened the door for her.

She grinned at him as she settled into the back seat. "Take it easy. Chrissy missed out on the meddling altogether tonight. Maybe Thanksgiving will be her turn."

Laughing, he closed her door.

As he began heading home, the city buzzed with activity. People wandered in and out of bars, celebrating the end of the workweek. Music spilled out of many of the venues, ranging from rock to jazz to alternative. Raucous laughter rang out of a comedy club.

Unhoused people huddled in dark corners, and Caden sighed as he walked past. As fall moved into winter, he would see more and more of them in the Emergency Department with many suffering from flu or frostbite. *The van has helped, but not enough.* He'd been in on the ground floor of the project that funded a van equipped to provide healthcare at shelters and encampments. He volunteered in the van several nights each month, and despite the challenges offered, he enjoyed offering care to the truly needy.

"Can you spare a dollar?" A figure emerged from a doorway with his hand out. Caden dug into his pocket and handed the man a Dunkin Donuts gift card. He always had several with him, knowing it would allow people to get a hot drink and something to fill their stomachs.

Walking helped him organize his thoughts and as he moved beyond the waterfront area, Caden's thoughts turned away from the people lacking housing, back to dinner. It had been fun, but also frustrating. His mother was amazing, but she still had a hard time realizing that, aside from Chrissy, her children were now adults who made their own decisions. Their house news had been a surprise, but it would be nice for them to have an escape from the brutal Boston winters. And he would make a point of going to visit them. It would be good for him to get away from the area occasionally. *I haven't taken a real vacation in years.* He shook his head. *Three years, to be exact.*

At the Healthy Living conference, one presentation highlighted keeping work and leisure in balance, because taking breaks makes for better employees. Caden was grateful for the reminder and would make it a point to emphasize it at the hospital and consider it more in his own life.

And there it was—thinking about the conference brought him back to Quinn. He wondered if she was home.

Chapter Two

O'Malley's

Caden

CADEN REACHED O'MALLEY'S PUB, his usual Friday-night spot to unwind with his friends Danny and Rob. He put his hand on the door, thought for a minute, then backed away, finding a quiet spot alongside the building.

Leaning against the brick wall, Caden pulled his phone out of his pocket and dialed Quinn's number. This time, he was ready with a response. "Hey Quinn, it's Caden. I thought you'd be home by now. Didn't the conference finish at noon? Hope you're not stuck in Boston traffic. Uh..." His mind went blank, and he berated himself. *Jesus, I can't even leave a decent message, and of course she knows I've called her twice now. Traffic? That's all I can come up with?*

To his surprise, her voicemail gave him the option of deleting his message and recording another. Relieved, he erased the message and ended the call. *My fucking word. What is wrong with me? We talked so easily yesterday.*

He sighed and shoved his phone back in his pocket. *Just let it go. She'll see my number and hopefully call back.*

Caden pushed open the heavy door to the pub and was immediately enveloped by the warm atmosphere. Dark wood wrapped around the walls and an Irish flag was proudly mounted over the bar. He had traveled to Ireland with his father and grandfather the summer he graduated from high school and O'Malley's made him think of his favorite of the many pubs they visited. It was quiet, but Caden knew the noise would increase as the night wore on. The dartboard on the far wall already had four guys cheering every time one of them threw a bullseye. Danny was at their usual spot, and they fist-bumped as Caden pulled up a stool. When the bartender slid his beer to him, he heaved a sigh before taking a swallow.

"Long day?" Danny asked.

"Chaotic as usual. I was supposed to be at workshops all week, but we ended up short-staffed, and I had to cover." And he'd lost the chance to spend more time with Quinn. But it hadn't all been bad. He smiled contentedly. "I delivered a baby this afternoon."

Danny's eyes widened. "Isn't that a little beyond your scope of expertise?"

"More than a little. The mom was ready to go when she arrived, and the obstetrician didn't get to the ER in time." He smiled again and took another swallow of his beer. "Those are the moments that make the job worthwhile. Is Robbie going to show tonight?"

"Nope. He texted me this afternoon, said something had come up."

Caden shook his head. "What's more important than tipping back a few at O'Malley's on Friday night?"

"I think it has something to do with their baby-making efforts."

Caden burst into laughter. Rob and his wife, Jennifer, had been trying to get pregnant for a few months. "So Robbie's getting lucky tonight, and you and I have each other. What's wrong with this picture?"

Danny chuckled with him. "Well, I'm going home to Brooke, and you know damn well you could take any woman here home with you."

Caden didn't dispute it, but he didn't rise to the bait either. He knew he was handsome enough. He'd been told plenty that women liked his firm jaw, dark curly hair, and deep-blue eyes. The guys gave him crap about dressing like he was a *GQ* model, but the truth was, he just liked nice clothes.

Time to change the subject. Danny worked for the media team of the New England Patriots, so Caden went that route. "On a different topic, how are the Patriots going to do this week? The docs in orthopedics have a pool going about when their first loss will be. They think the team's playing over its head."

Danny straightened to his full height, which was several inches shorter than Caden, and took a long swallow of his beer before shaking his head in disgust. His fiery temper matched his red hair, and he was fiercely competitive. "We are going to be just fine. Everybody thought we were sunk after our quarterback moved on. It's taken some time, but our rookie is setting records this year. Over its head, my ass."

Caden downed his beer, chuckling. "It's so much fun to get you going." They grew up playing hockey together, and Danny's loyalty had made him Caden's favorite teammate. They still spent their winters playing in an amateur hockey league. "How soon are we going to have ice to skate on?"

"It's been so mild, probably not until just before Thanksgiving." After the server brought the next round, Danny jutted his chin to the right. "There's a hot lady over there checking you out. You won't have to go home alone."

Turning his head slightly, Caden saw the woman clearly ogling him. He turned back to Danny. "Not my type."

"Jesus, what is your type? What's it been—a year since you've been with a woman? What do you want?"

Caden paused before responding, studying the liquid in the bottle. Finally, he said, softly, "I want what you have with Brooke, what Robbie has with Jennifer. I want a partner to go through life with. I found nothing close to that in a year and a half of matches from dating apps." His sex life had been very active during his online-dating time, but he was one and done with all of them, not interested in developing a relationship. A year ago, the realization hit that the one-night stands weren't good for his psyche. He withdrew from the dating world altogether after that. "And I want kids."

In the silence that followed, Caden raised his eyes and could see Danny considering his words. It was the first time he'd articulated his feelings this clearly to his friend.

Danny leaned in closer and hissed, "She's not a match from an app. She's right here! Ten feet away!"

"Nah, she's looking at me like I'm a piece of meat. She only wants to get laid."

Danny shook his head. "Man, when did you become so sensitive?"

"Wow. I finally get why women don't like being looked up and down," Caden quipped. He played with the label on his beer bottle. "I met a woman at the conference yesterday." He turned to look at Danny. "She's a nurse in New Hampshire, near where Claire lives."

Danny raised his eyebrows. "That's convenient. You could see her when you visit Claire."

"Yeah, that's my thinking. I kind of invited her to dinner when the baby is born. She was easy to talk to. I'm pissed I couldn't make it back to the conference today." He picked up his phone, opened the photos, and found the one Quinn had sent him that morning. Her dark hair was long and wavy, her eyes a warm brown, and he gazed at it for a second before sliding the phone toward Danny.

"She's pretty."

"Yeah. I don't know—there was this attraction between us. Well, *I'm* attracted. Not sure about her."

"It's only a two-hour drive. You could go up there anytime."

"I know." Caden picked up his phone and slid it back into his pocket.

Danny sighed and looked at his watch. "I need to head home."

Caden finished his beer in one last swallow, then said, "Do me a favor. Keep this between us."

"Not even Robbie?"

Caden nodded. "Or Brooke."

Danny's face fell. Caden knew he had no secrets from his wife.

"Hey," Caden said. "I don't know what I'm going to do, and I don't want to be bugged about it. Or have to explain if I do nothing."

"Brooke won't say anything, you know that. I don't like to keep things from her."

Caden sighed. Brooke and Danny were his closest friends. He was their son's godfather, and they would do anything for him. "Okay, if you feel the need, you can tell Brooke. But emphasize that I may not pursue it. I'm not sure if I want to open myself up." Standing to leave, he paused and met Danny's eyes. "It felt good to have a spark of attraction. First one in a long time."

They walked out the door, and Danny said, "This is when I'm jealous of you. Wish I lived close enough to walk home."

"Proximity to O'Malley's was the deciding factor when I bought the brownstone. You calling an Uber?"

"Nah, I'm sober enough to wrangle my way on the T. I'm on the road next week, so see you in two." They fist-bumped, and just before they parted, he said, "Hey, Cade. It's been three years since Mary fucked you over. Take the chance."

"Are you writing cards for Hallmark now?" Caden smirked as he walked away.

Chapter Three

Hanover

Quinn

QUINN MICHAELS UNLOCKED THE door to her town house and scooped up the large marmalade-colored cat who'd begun rubbing insistently against her legs the second she entered. She buried her face in his fur. "Hi, Max, did you miss me? Huh, did you miss me?"

Max put up with being held for a few minutes before squirming out of her arms to run to his dish in the kitchen, where he meowed aggressively until Quinn dumped some food into the bowl and refreshed his water.

Quinn poured herself a glass of wine, went back to the living room, and kneeled in front of the fireplace. She crumpled some newspaper to add to the kindling she had arranged before she left for Boston the previous Sunday. She lit a match and touched it to the paper, and the flames flickered to life. When they seemed strong enough, she gently laid a log on top.

Quinn stood, stretching her arms up and turning her head from side to side, trying to work out the kinks caused by her drive from Boston to Hanover, which rush-hour traffic had stretched from its usual two hours to three and a half. She pulled the elastic band from her ponytail, allowing her dark, wavy hair to cascade over her shoulders.

Her eyes landed on the pile of newly purchased stuff she had dropped near the door when Max insisted on being picked up. Walking back to the entry, she searched through the bags from her shopping spree at Quincy Market. Finally, she reached into one and pulled out a silk-screened print that read, "Wan-der-lust, noun, a strong desire to travel."

She placed it on the mantle and stepped back, assessing the look with a critical eye. "Yes! That's what was missing. I knew as soon as I saw it." Pleased, she picked up her wineglass and sat on the couch.

Quinn looked around the living room with its cream-colored walls and the tawny drapes framing a large window. She smiled and ran her hand over the velvet of her dark green sofa.

As much as I enjoy traveling, I truly love it here. The view out that window isn't great, but my deck off the dining area makes up for it. Trees surrounded the housing complex on three sides, and Quinn's deck overlooked a babbling stream. *Probably won't be sitting out there again until spring, but I enjoyed it during the summer.*

The town house had been hers for two years, and she'd been slowly furnishing it to reflect her taste. For the first time, at twenty-nine, Quinn lived in a place she loved.

During college in Virginia, and for a year after graduation, she had shared an apartment with two other women, and their furniture had been makeshift. Quinn left it all behind when she moved to Seattle and rented a furnished apartment during her three years there. Now, her life in Hanover was truly her own. She chuckled to herself. *It's sinful how much pleasure I get from living here and knowing it's mine.*

She leaned back and brought her legs onto the sofa, stretching out to relax as she sipped her wine, then picked up the remote and turned on her favorite cooking show. Mindless entertainment was always at the top of her agenda on Fridays, and after the week she'd had in Boston, Quinn needed it more than ever.

Quinn had been in Boston for a conference on Healthy Living in the Workplace. She had recently become the wellness coordinator for her ward at Dartmouth Hitchcock Hospital in New Hampshire, where she worked as a nurse, and wanted to do a better job than the former coordinator.

But the conference wasn't all work. She'd also run into Sam Carpenter, her high school boyfriend, who she hadn't seen in ten years. Which had been... interesting.

Max sauntered back to the living room and stood looking at her.

"Do you think it's kitty time? I think you're right. Come on up. I need some kitty snuggles." Max jumped on her chest, and Quinn stroked his fur, listening to his very loud purring. Snuggling him always helped her relax, which she needed after a week spent surrounded by people. It went against her introverted soul to have so many days in a row with no alone time.

"Let me tell you about my week. You expected me back on Wednesday, didn't you? Sorry about that, but my boss found room for me in another conference in Cambridge, so I had to stay longer."

Max started kneading his paws on her sweater.

"I know, I know. I was intimidated as hell going to a second conference where I didn't know anyone." Quinn was confident in her professional skills, and she'd cultivated a strong circle of friends since her move to New Hampshire, but being in unfamiliar surroundings or with strangers resurrected echoes of the shy, awkward teenager she had been. "The very first day..."

Her phone rang with her friend Angie's ringtone. Quinn chuckled. *I knew she'd call after she read my text.* She answered and held the phone away from her ear.

"Girlfriend!" Angie's screech startled Max, and he jumped to the floor, taking off for the kitchen. "I need details! You can't leave me hanging with a message like that."

Quinn sighed. She had sent Angie a text before leaving Boston telling her she was going to spend more time with Sam after the conference.

"We spent time together after you left, and he convinced me his relationship with Norah is over. We both want to get reacquainted."

"Uh-huh. What did you do during this time you spent together?"

"We had dinner, we rode to Cambridge together..."

Angie interrupted her. "Dammit, I need to hang up. There's some kind of big dispute going on between my kids. But we're not done. I want to hear all about the *time* you spent together!"

She hung up, and Quinn chuckled. She was lucky to have Angie as one of her closest friends, dramatic or not. They had become friends during classes for the advanced-degree program they were pursuing. Since they lived hours away from each other, they lived off phone calls until they could get together in person. She'd gotten to spend time with Angie at the conference this past week, but they wouldn't be together again in person until the end of January.

Max tentatively walked back to the couch, looking up plaintively, and Quinn said, "It's safe. You can come back up." After he resettled on her chest, she relaxed again. "So, did you hear that? The first day of the conference, the boy I dated in high school sat next to me. His name is Sam. We met when I was a sophomore, and he became my best friend. We started dating my junior year and became everything to each other." She took a swallow of her wine. "My first love. But our love didn't survive after I left for college."

Realizing her wineglass was empty, she shifted the cat off her, murmuring an apology, and went to the kitchen to refill it. Max didn't leave her side, however, waiting until she sat back down to jump right back up to his spot on top of her.

Quinn smiled and petted him. "We went to dinner the first night because he wanted to catch up, and it turns out he lives near here. I thought dinner would be it, and I'd never see him again, but we ended up spending time together every day. I didn't realize how much I missed him." *Yeah, boy, did we spend time together, especially this afternoon.* Her body tingled as she thought about Sam's touch. Then she remembered how he'd told her during the week that the mother of his child was moving out while he was at the conference. He'd been a mess those first few days.

Max shifted a bit, bringing her back.

"Was he needy? Of course. You know me, Max—I'm always drawn to those damn needy guys."

Max reached his paw up to her face.

"Yeah, kinda like you, big guy." Quinn stroked his fur. "What now, you wonder? Will you get to meet him? You may. We're going to see where things lead." She paused. "No, I won't be leaving you alone all the time. He has a daughter, and I'll only see him while she's with her mother. I know it's awfully soon after their breakup, but according to him, it's been coming for a long time. No, he wouldn't bullshit me about something that serious."

At least, she hoped he wouldn't.

Max jumped down, giving Quinn the chance to pick up her phone. She took another sip of wine as she opened her photos to look at the selfie she had taken with Sam the night before at an Italian restaurant in Boston's North End. Sam's hair was light brown, and his icy-blue eyes glowed in sharp contrast to the dark brown of Quinn's eyes. Their smiles were wide, reflecting their happiness at having reconnected.

It was good to reconnect. In every way.

She closed the photo app and found five text messages from Sam.

> *Sam: Hope you got home okay.*

> *Sam: Bought those inflatable mattresses we talked about.*

> *Sam: I miss you.*

Sam: I was hoping to hear from you tonight.

Sam: Talk tomorrow?

She shook her head, thinking of high school when they texted each other all the time, then put down her wineglass.

Quinn: I'm home and heading to bed. Catch up tomorrow.

As she closed the messages, she noticed two missed calls. *Probably Mom, wanting to chat about my trip.* But when she looked at the list of recent calls, it surprised her to see both calls had come from private numbers. No voicemail, though.

Quinn shrugged and drained her wineglass.

If they couldn't leave a message, I guess they didn't really want to talk to me.

Chapter Four

Drinks With Ashley

Quinn

QUINN WOKE UP AFTER nine, savoring the thought of having nothing to do for the entire day. She sat up and glanced fondly around her bedroom, focusing on the accent wall she and her father had finished just before he and her mother left to spend the winter in Florida.

I love the contrast of the natural wood against the dark walls. Dad thought I'd tire of that deep green, but the wall, along with the white curtains and headboard, makes it all work perfectly. She stretched, happy to have slept in her own bed.

Quinn was an only child and relished the close relationship she had with her parents. Her mother had grown to be one of her best friends and closest confidantes. Quinn shared everything with her. *What am I going to tell her about Sam?* Her parents had a front-row seat to her heartbreak ten years earlier and might not react well to Quinn opening herself up to that again. *I'm not going to rush to tell Mom that I saw him, or that I'm going to see him again.* She shivered and pulled the covers up to her chin. *It wasn't only me that was hurt when he disappeared.* No, her parents would not like the idea of Sam being back in her life.

Her dad, Hank, was not as interested in dissecting every detail of her life, but he was there whenever Quinn needed him. His fingerprints were everywhere in the townhouse, the walls he'd helped her paint, the backsplash in the kitchen and tile floor in the bathroom. *I couldn't have gotten as much done in two years without his help.* She missed her parents during the time they spent in Florida and couldn't wait until they were back in Vermont for Christmas.

Quinn picked up her phone to check the weather and found three more texts from Sam.

Sam: Hey

> *Sam: Waiting for Norah to get here with Piper*

> *Sam: They're here*

She wondered how it had gone for him seeing Norah for the first time since Monday, when she had announced she was moving out.

> *Quinn: Hope you have a good few days with your daughter.*

Quinn put the phone down and groaned, remembering she needed to work on her final research paper for her course. It was the last project of the semester and due in less than a month. Still, she dressed in her workout clothes. *I'm going for a run first. There won't be many more mild days like this.*

Quinn drove to downtown Hanover, finding a place to park a block from the main street. She started on her favorite route, which took her through the vibrant Dartmouth campus and into residential neighborhoods filled with well-landscaped colonial and Victorian homes, many bustling with fall decor. Quinn knew that, in a few short weeks, the orange pumpkins and yellow leaves would give way to twinkling white lights and the reds and greens of Christmas decorations.

Someday, I'm going to own one of these houses.

Sam's texts entered her mind, warming her soul. Quinn had not been on a date in over two years, having made the choice to stop searching for a partner after numerous one-night stands and two long-term relationships in which she'd been treated poorly. Sam had been the only man—just a boy at the time, really—who had treated her well. *Until the end, when he broke my heart and shattered my self-esteem.* Running into him in Boston had been totally unexpected, but their time together during the week had finally provided both of them with closure about the way their relationship had ended ten years earlier.

It had also led to them rekindling their physical relationship and deciding to continue seeing each other after they returned home.

Quinn wasn't without reservations about this plan. As her feet pounded the pavement, she thought about how good those two years without men had been for her. She became more comfortable with herself, developed a few strong female friendships, and could say with confidence that she loved her life. Opening herself up again to anyone was frightening, much less someone who'd hurt her before. She simply hoped Sam was being honest when he told her his relationship with Norah was over. But then she remembered the feel of his arm over her shoulder, pulling her close to him as they walked along the streets of Boston. The warmth of the kisses they shared on that walk, the intimacy they'd shared in her hotel room, made her realize she didn't want to spend her life alone.

Almost back on the Dartmouth campus, she slowed to watch a dad throwing a football with his young son. The boy's return pass sailed out of control and landed at Quinn's feet. She scooped it up and tossed it to the dad as the boy came running over.

"I'm so sorry," the boy panted. "The ball didn't hit you, did it?"

She smiled. "No, I'm fine."

The boy sprinted back onto his lawn, caught his dad's return pass, and started running with the ball. The dad ran after him then tackled him, both laughing.

I love running on this route. The family vibe is overwhelming.

Quinn had made it back to Main Street, finishing the five-mile loop by running past restaurants, coffee shops, and a bookstore with racks of logo wear displayed on the sidewalk. She leaned against her car to catch her breath, and when her heartbeat returned to normal, she grabbed her wallet to walk back to the flower shop that had caught her eye a few blocks before.

At home, she carried a bouquet of fall blossoms to her dining area and her latest furniture purchase, a table big enough to accommodate the group of women Quinn came together with once a month to share a meal. Her turn to host would be in a couple of months, and she was looking forward to it. Placing the flowers in the center of the table, she looked at Max. "I've put it off as long as I can. I'm going to shower, then I *must* start working on my paper."

Quinn found several more messages from Sam as she sat down to study, and she sent him a quick text letting him know she was working on her research paper and turning off her phone to avoid interruptions. It was late afternoon before she pushed back from the table and stretched her arms in front of her, then shut off her laptop.

With a sigh, she powered up her phone and sent Sam a message.

> Quinn: Going out to dinner with a friend. Hope you and Piper have a nice evening.

She walked into the Sidecar, a bar and grill across the river in Vermont, where she was meeting Ashley, her closest friend at the hospital. They were both twenty-nine and had been happily single until Ash started dating an X-ray technologist. Unsurprisingly, Ash was late, probably because of said X-ray tech. Quinn ordered their usual—two margaritas and a plate of nachos—as soon as she sat down and settled in to wait.

A few minutes after the food and drinks arrived, Ashley dashed in, slid into a chair, and pushed her blond hair out of her face. "I'm sorry I'm late!" She took a swallow of her drink, then grinned at Quinn. "I missed you! The ward's not the same when you're gone. How was your week in the big city? It must have thrilled you to be there for two extra days! I know you were excited to be in Boston but then adding in a college campus? *Ooh-la-la!* Any cute grad students?"

Quinn laughed. "You know me too well. It was great. You won't believe what happened the first day at Harvard. I was early..."

Ashley smirked. "Of course you were. That goes without saying."

Quinn rolled her eyes. "Yes, thank you. Anyway, I stopped at a kiosk to buy a chai, and when I stepped out of line, this kid rushed by at a dead run and knocked it out of my hand. I didn't have time to wait for another one, so I went to the lecture hall, and ten minutes later, I'm looking at my phone when this voice behind me says, 'I bought you a replacement.'" Quinn lowered her voice to imitate Caden's deep tone, and Ashley gasped with delight.

Quinn continued. "I turned around to see this gorgeous—seriously, drop-dead gorgeous—guy standing there, holding two cups. He sat next to me. We chatted the whole day and had lunch together. He's a doctor at Mass General and has a sister who lives in Hanover. She's on the accounting team at the hospital."

Ashley's face broke into a huge smile. "The mythical tall, dark, and handsome man!" Quinn chuckled—it was one of their running jokes. "But a sister in Hanover? That's convenient. He could visit her and have a date with you."

Quinn nodded. "She's pregnant, and he mentioned he'll be coming up when she has the baby. He asked if I'd go to dinner with him so he didn't have to spend all his time here oohing and aahing over the newborn."

"Cool." Ashley sipped her drink.

"Well, maybe not. Because on the very first day of the conference, Sam Carpenter, my high school boyfriend, sat next to me. I've told you about him."

Ashley sat back, surprise wiping the smile from her face. "No shit."

"Yup." Quinn's cheeks warmed. "We saw each other several times during the week."

Ashley looked at her expectantly. "And what happened? You're blushing so much you look like a ripe tomato."

Quinn hesitated, but she needed to tell someone. *Might as well get it out now.* She took a drink of her margarita, snaking her tongue out to lick the salt on the rim, then leaned in, catching Ashley's eye and silently urging her to come closer. "We had sex the last night in Boston. And actually, again yesterday after the conference ended. It was amazing." Remembering her time in bed with Sam started her body tingling, and she grinned at the shock in Ashley's eyes. "We're going to see where this can go. He only lives about twenty miles from here."

Ashley leaned back again. "Whoa. After all the negative things you told me about him?"

Quinn sighed. "I know." She toyed with a lock of hair. "That was a defense mechanism. Years ago, I concentrated on his flaws to get over him. Then it became a habit to focus on the negatives when I thought about him. From the first dinner we shared, I started remembering all the sweet things about him." Her phone buzzed, and she dug it out of her pocket. It was a text from Sam wishing her good night. She showed the phone screen to Ashley. "He's sent several texts since yesterday. It's kind of flattering."

"Several?" Ashley's eyes opened wide as she took in the text convo. "You're okay with so much attention, Miss Independent?" All of Quinn's friends knew why she'd been single for two years.

She shrugged. "For now, anyway. I'm sure when he's working, and the newness has worn off, it will let up."

"Didn't you tell me once he lives with someone and has a child?" Ashley never pulled her punches.

"He has a daughter named Piper, and he was living with her mother. She moved out while Sam was in Boston."

"Quinn..." The concern in Ashley's voice was obvious. "He's just out of a relationship. Is this a good idea?"

"I know." Quinn briefly shared the details Sam had told her about his relationship with Norah and how it had been falling apart for several years. When she finished, she sighed. "I'm going in with my eyes wide-open. It may not last, but my attraction to him, both physically and emotionally, is wicked strong."

She noted Ashley's look of suspicion. "I know, I know, but I promise, eyes wide-open. You didn't know me when I was in a relationship, but I assure you, I had blinders on back then. I've worked hard since I moved here to get rid of them." Quinn flashed her a sly grin. "And if it doesn't work out, at least I will have had some mind-blowing sex in the meantime."

Ashley chuckled, but Quinn still read the wariness in her eyes. *Time to switch up the discussion.* Quinn ordered additional drinks and said, "Let me tell you some ideas I brought back from Boston."

While they finished the nachos, Quinn shared more information about the conference, and Ashley updated her about the hospital ward during her absence. Their second drinks were almost gone when Ashley mused, "It's kind of interesting you told me about the tall, dark, and handsome doctor before you even mentioned Sam."

Quinn frowned. "Because you asked me if I saw any cute men at Harvard. And I did!"

Ashley raised her eyebrows. "Okay. What will you do if *he* calls while you're sort of dating Sam?"

"Come on." Quinn shook her head. "Guys like that never follow through. I won't hear from him again." She pushed her chair back and stood. "I need to see where this is going with Sam."

Ashley rose from the table. "I get that. I think."

They hugged, and Quinn smiled. "Don't worry about me. I'll be fine."

Despite Quinn's confidence, Ashley's words fueled the doubt simmering below the surface.

Am I going to end up getting hurt again? No. I think I've learned enough about protecting my heart to end it before that happens.

I hope.

Chapter Five

Swimming With Izzy

Quinn

QUINN HAD BARELY OPENED her eyes on Wednesday morning when butterflies started doing somersaults in her stomach. In just a few short hours, she was going to present the mentoring program she'd developed to the hospital's wellness coordinators.

It's an excellent program, and we need it. And I need to remember I'm not a fifteen-year-old afraid to speak in front of strangers.

She yawned. Between putting the finishing touches on her presentation and texting with Sam, she had stayed up way too late. Sam had been overwhelming her with messages.

He must have a lot more open time than I do. My phone's in my pocket all day, and I barely look at it.

Before leaving Boston, they had agreed to get together on Wednesday. Quinn asked him the night before about meeting at a new restaurant, but he had declined, inviting her to come to his house in Thetford, Vermont, instead. It was only about twenty miles away, and she was excited to see him again, so she was sure some of the morning's butterflies were related to Sam.

When Quinn started her car, a warning appeared on the dashboard, letting her know the roads could be icy, a jarring reminder that the temperatures were dropping. Many New Englanders dreaded November, but Quinn liked it, relishing the change of season. The colored leaves of fall would fade away to usher in the holiday season. She lit a fire in her fireplace nearly every night, enjoying the cozy feel it gave the town house, and she looked forward to the first snowfall like a ten-year-old hoping for a snow day.

Quinn arrived at the community center and, as always, thought about how grateful she was for the large indoor pool housed there. Jumping into the water and pounding out laps was her favorite way to work away stress. Inside, she changed from leggings and a sweatshirt to her black bathing suit and pulled her hair into a ponytail. Walking out to the pool deck,

Quinn waved at the girl, catching her breath while hanging on the side of the pool.

"Hey, Izzy," Quinn said. "What are you doing here at five thirty?"

"Hey, Quinn." Izzy flexed her neck. "Couldn't sleep, and I can't come in the evenings because I have theater rehearsals every night." She grinned. "Wanna race?"

"Give me ten minutes to warm up." Quinn jumped into the pool and let the water wash away her sleepiness.

And she would have to be at her best to give Izzy a good race—that was how they had met the prior spring, after weeks of swimming in adjacent lanes. One day, the girl had approached her, introducing herself as Isabella Wiley. "You're the strongest swimmer here. Do you race?"

Quinn had smiled as she replied, "I did in high school, but that was years ago. I'm hardly the strongest."

"I'm looking for someone to help me improve my turns. The only people better than you are on the college team, and I can't ask them." She explained she was trying to make the college swim team as a walk-on and had failed her first year, but she wasn't about to give up.

Quinn worked with the younger woman twice a week until Izzy went home for the summer. They had exchanged numbers, and to Quinn's surprise, Izzy started texting her in early July. Izzy told her how training was going and made Quinn laugh with descriptions of her dates. They started swimming together again when classes resumed in the fall and went out to dinner every other week.

One night, after several glasses of wine, Izzy told Quinn, "I only have brothers. You're my honorary big sister."

Quinn's heart had nearly burst. "I'm an only child, and I'd have loved a little sister like you." From then on, their friendship had been even more precious to her.

After ten minutes of warm-up, Quinn felt as ready as she'd ever be. "Okay, Izzy. What are we going to do today?" She rested against the edge of the pool, waiting for Izzy to select a stroke for their race.

"Let's go with the butterfly. Four laps."

Quinn groaned. "I don't know why I let you choose. You always pick the same thing."

"Because the butterfly is where I fell short in tryouts. I *will* shave those seconds off my time."

"Okay, butterfly. I admire your determination—but remember, I'll never let you win."

"I should hope not!"

One of the other early-morning swimmers counted down from three to start the race, and they were off. As they cut through the water, Quinn noted Izzy was matching her stroke for stroke until they were almost at the end. With a last burst of power, Quinn pulled ahead to finish seconds before Izzy.

They clung to the side of the pool, gasping for air. When Izzy could talk, she said, "Almost, Quinn, almost. The day's going to come when I beat your ass."

Quinn laughed, still short of breath. "There's not a doubt in my mind, Izzy. That day is coming. Especially if you keep making me do the butterfly."

They swam a few more laps together before Quinn noticed the time. "I need to get moving. I have an important meeting this morning."

While Quinn dried her hair in the locker room, Izzy asked, "Do you want to come to my theater performance? It's a Christmas variety show." She laughed. "Does that sound lame? It's the first week in December."

Quinn smiled. "Yeah, I'd like that. A way to get into the Christmas spirit."

Izzy searched her bag and handed her two tickets to Quinn. "You can bring a date." She grinned. She knew Quinn hadn't had a date in over two years.

But Izzy didn't know things might change on that front. "Thanks!" Quinn winked at Izzy. "You never know..."

Quinn checked in on the ward, then made her way to the small auditorium on the main floor of the hospital. It was Quinn's first meeting with the other coordinators. Her presentation on the mentorship program was ready, and she hoped the hospital would let her ward be the pilot for it.

Quinn looked at the other attendees, and while she saw familiar faces from the hallways, there was no one she knew personally. She slid into an empty seat on the aisle near the stage, giving her easy access when it was her turn to present.

She was giving her notes a final glance when she sensed someone standing near her. Quinn turned her head and was greeted by a man in a white coat.

"Hi. Can I squeeze by you?" He pointed to an open seat beyond her.

She nodded and stood to let him pass.

He entered the row and sat down, leaving an empty seat between them. He sighed and shook his head. "Man, I hate these things. Not sure why I thought being the wellness coordinator for my department was a good idea." He looked at Quinn. "Are you new? I don't remember seeing you here before."

"This is my first meeting. I've been the wellness coordinator on the fourth-floor medical ward for about a month. What should I expect today?" The HR director had given her an overview, but she liked to hear the perspective of other people.

"In the past, there'd be announcements and then Q and A. Pretty routine. This chick is new, and I have no idea what she will do. It sounds like she intends to meet more often."

Quinn's eyebrows went up in surprise at his use of the word *chick*.

"Oh, man." He shook his head. "Sorry about that. I'm such a cretin." His grin told Quinn he really wasn't sorry at all. "There's also a presentation this morning—another way to prolong the agony."

Quinn's breath caught. *I hope everyone doesn't feel that way.*

The director stepped to the podium. "Good morning. I'm Laurel Bennett, and I'm pleased to welcome you. I know you have questions, and I encourage you to submit them online. We have a presentation this morning by Quinn Michaels, one of our newest wellness coordinators. Quinn has put together a mentoring program based on information she learned at a recent Healthy Living conference."

Quinn stood, feeling everyone's eyes on her as she walked to the stage. She started her PowerPoint presentation, gaining confidence as she moved through the slides. "As we all know, the hospital has a three-month orientation program for new hires. At the end of that time, they are let loose with no planned means of support. Our culture is not always welcoming, and it can take new hires a long time before they find a comfort level. I should add, this is not unique to our hospital."

Quinn stopped to take a sip of water. People were nodding, which was good. "I'm proposing a year-long mentorship that would start after orientation. Mentor and mentee will meet twice monthly for the first three months, then once a month for the next nine. These will be in-person meetings conducted at a mutually agreed-upon time outside of the workday."

Quinn continued through the slides, then asked for questions. Unsurprisingly, the first was whether the mentors would be compensated, and she nodded. "Both mentor and mentee will be paid for their meeting time, and the mentor will receive a monthly stipend. The mentee will receive a bump in pay when the program is completed."

The questions continued. One doctor asked how the program would affect their budgets and when the program would start. Laurel replied the mentor program did not currently have funding and could not be implemented for six to twelve months.

Quinn spoke up, addressing Laurel directly. "Begging your pardon, ma'am, but all departments have personal development budgets that could be used for this." She gave statistics on the increase in retention at hospitals with similar programs. "Employee retention is one of our biggest and most costly problems." In the wake of that point, Quinn had time to cite the dollars lost when employees left in their first year and the professional-development budgets for various departments before the meeting ended. She felt she'd made her point and hoped Laurel agreed.

Quinn stepped off the stage, making her way through the professionals eager to return to their regular work. Several of them congratulated her and acknowledged how desperately the mentor program was needed. When she reached the seat where she'd left her bag, the doctor who had spoken to her earlier was waiting.

"That wasn't agony at all." He smiled with sincerity this time. "You were a badass up there. Hope it gains some traction."

"Thank you." Quinn smiled to herself. *I was smooth and sure of myself. Another step away from that insecure teenager.*

A week later, Quinn had Wednesday off and started her day by meeting Izzy at the pool. After they raced, with Quinn winning again, Izzy asked if Quinn had time to grab a cup of coffee with her.

Quinn arrived at the coffee shop first and took a deep breath, savoring the scents of fall. An apple pie had just come out of the oven, and the blend of cinnamon, clove, and apple turned the air intoxicating. Quinn considered purchasing the pie but restrained herself, instead ordering a pumpkin-spice latte and a cranberry scone.

She sat at a booth and took a swallow of the latte, glad coffee with Izzy would take her mind off what she was planning to do that night.

Quinn had just finished her scone when Izzy, wrapped in a shawl against the chill, slid into the booth across from her with a coffee and a muffin. She pulled off her white beanie, allowing short strawberry blond curls to wreathe her face.

"Quinn, do you think I'm wasting my time?"

Quinn stared at Izzy's worried face. "In what way? You're carrying eighteen credits, taking part in theater productions, lifeguarding... Did I leave anything out? Where's a wasted minute?"

"Trying to make the swim team." Izzy sighed. "I feel like it's useless to spend all this time training. That I won't make it."

"Oh, sweetie, I don't know. I never swam at the collegiate level, so I don't know what makes you competitive." Quinn paused. "Have you spoken to the coach?"

"Last spring when he told me I didn't make the team. He said I only missed it by a few seconds." Izzy began absentmindedly shredding her muffin. "There are several seniors leaving the team this year, but who knows how many hotshot freshmen there will be."

"Do you enjoy swimming?"

Izzy nodded.

"Then keep doing it. You're going to do something for exercise, and you told me swimming is your favorite. Don't give it up. Maybe..." Quinn stopped and gave her friend a gentle smile. "Maybe just don't put so much pressure on yourself. Let it be fun."

Izzy pulled her shawl tighter. "I feel like I've forgotten how to have fun."

Boy, does that sound familiar. Quinn sipped her coffee. "I'm too young to be giving you the mom lecture about how this is the best time of your life. Plus, you're at the hardest point of the semester. I can remember feeling the same way when I was in college."

Izzy looked down at the mangled muffin. "What a mess I've made. I know you're right. Now that you've mentioned it, I remember feeling the same way in the spring." She sighed and picked up her fork to eat the pieces of her muffin.

Quinn nodded, hoping Izzy would cut herself some slack going forward. Then Izzy surprised her by asking, "What about you? Something's bugging you. I could tell when you walked into the pool."

Busted. "I have to do something difficult tonight." Quinn could see the question in Izzy's eyes and knew she'd have to explain. "You know how I don't date?"

Izzy nodded.

"I've been seeing someone for the last couple of weeks, and I'm going to end it. He's going to be upset."

Izzy scoffed. "After two weeks? That's nothing."

Quinn wished it were that simple. "We have history. It goes back a long time."

"That's intriguing." Izzy sipped her coffee.

"Someday I'll tell you all about it, but not this morning."

Izzy nodded. "If it goes back longer than two weeks, did you at least... you know, get together?"

Quinn blushed, and Izzy pounced on it.

"You did!" Izzy hooted. "Does this mean your moratorium on dating is over?"

Quinn chuckled and stood. "I have an appointment to get my snow tires put on. I'll see you after Thanksgiving."

Izzy waved goodbye, and Quinn took her coffee and headed out to her car.

Am I going to start dating again? Have I been dating Sam? That's not how I thought of it. We were just two friends catching up. And then we carried it a little further.

Quinn's body tingled with the memory of the wild sex with Sam in Boston. *Okay, a lot further.* Quinn had gone to Sam's house three times since the conference, and they'd slept together on Saturday night. It had been... fine, although not as good as Boston.

The pleasurable tingles faded as she thought about what had happened after. *God, I feel so humiliated about that. And I know I shouldn't. It's Sam's problem, not mine. But it sure as hell proved that he's not over Norah.*

But tonight, he and I will be over, for better or for worse. She hoped they would still be friends afterward.

Chapter Six

The Handsome Doctor Texts

Caden

CADEN WAS THE FIRST to arrive at O'Malley's on Friday night, two weeks after he'd tried to call Quinn following the conference. Two weeks since she hadn't called him back.

The bartender asked, "Where are your buddies tonight?" He slid Caden's beer toward him.

As he said this, Robbie came in and signaled for a beer.

Caden smiled at Robbie and then told him and the bartender, "Danny's tied up at work, said he'd be late but not to leave." After nodding at the bartender, Caden turned to Robbie. "I was late because of a staff meeting. What's your excuse?"

Robbie took a long swallow of the beer that had appeared in front of him, then he put the glass down and stared at it. "Operation Baby-Making two weeks ago didn't take. Jenny found out this morning." He shrugged. "I went home to check on her. She's out with Brooke now."

"Oh man, I'm sorry. You both must be disappointed."

Robbie nodded. "Yeah. But now we get to try some more. It's early. She only went off the pill a few months ago." He flashed a faint smile. "But a heads-up. I predict Danny will be very worked up tonight. A colleague who follows the police logs picked up something about a Patriots player getting arrested."

They relaxed and drank their beers, watching a college basketball game on the television over the bar until both of their phones dinged at the same time.

> *Brooke: Will one of you make sure Danny gets home okay?*

Caden looked at Robbie. "Which one of us is going to be his babysitter?"

Robbie sighed. "I will. I'm meeting with one of my *guardian ad litem* kids in the morning, so I'm going to take it easy tonight."

Caden replied to Brooke, letting her know Rob would look out for Danny.

"Hey," Robbie said. "That reminds me—do you have your number masked on your phone? The texts I've gotten from you recently all say they're from a private number."

Frowning, Caden put down his glass. "Do you know when that started?"

Robbie looked through his texts. "The last one I got with your name was... about two weeks ago." He looked a little more closely. "Two weeks ago yesterday, to be exact."

Caden checked his phone's settings. "Shit! I changed it the next morning because I was making calls to find someone to cover a shift. I mask it because people don't answer if they see my name because they know I want them to come to work." He snorted. "For all the good it does. Half the time, they won't answer a call from a private number either. Damn, damn, damn!" He changed the setting and shoved the phone into his pocket.

Robbie shrugged. "It's no big deal. I always knew it was you, and probably Danny did, too."

Yeah, but Quinn didn't. Caden guzzled the rest of his beer. "I can't believe I was so stupid." *No wonder she didn't call me back. I'm an idiot.* He ordered another drink.

Danny stormed through the door a few minutes later, his face like a thundercloud. He got to the bar, grasped the beer the bartender held out to him, and said, "Keep 'em coming." After draining the glass, he finally looked at his friends. "You won't believe my day. Our star running back is an imbecile."

"The all-star rookie kid?" Caden asked.

Danny huffed. "Ran a red light last night and blew three times the legal limit. Who *does* that? Drinks three times the legal limit and then *drives a car*?"

The bartender slid a full glass across the bar, and Danny took another long swallow.

"There were times we drank that much," Caden mused. "We were lucky. We always had public transportation."

"Or one of us stayed sober," Robbie added.

Danny nodded his head vigorously. "Exactly. *Anyone* would have driven him last night. It's a PR nightmare. We spent all day trying to deal with it, and we're not done. He acted like an arrogant idiot. Got mouthy with the cops, resisted arrest, you name it. A nightmare!"

The ranting continued over the next hour, as Danny downed several more beers. When he finally left them for the restroom, Caden looked at Robbie. "You knew all that?"

Robbie grimaced. "Most of it. Danny's going to have his work cut out for him. We should get him out of here."

Caden nodded.

On Danny's return, Robbie said, "It's getting late. We should head out."

Danny shook his head and ordered another round for the three of them. Robbie sighed and didn't touch his.

"Come on now. Don't let me drink alone." Danny had finished his beer and ordered shots for himself and Caden. Caden took his and watched a grin flash across Danny's face before he asked, "Which one of you yahoos is babysitting me tonight?"

Drunk Danny was always a handful—and he knew it.

Robbie raised his hand. "That would be me. And I have stuff to do in the morning, so we need to wrap this up."

Danny burped. "I figured." He looked at Caden. "Like I said, I think you bought that damn brownstone, so you'd be close to the bar and not have to make sure I get home. I need to hit the can first."

Caden grinned at Robbie. "He may have a point. I'm glad it's you tonight. Are you taking the T?"

"Hell no, I'm not wrestling him on the subway. I'll call an Uber. And it's a good thing you can walk home. You're almost as drunk as he is."

Caden got to his feet, wobbling a bit. "You might be right."

As they waited outside for the rideshare Robbie had called, Danny looked at Caden. "Have you called that nurse yet?" His voice was only a little slurred.

Caden glared at him.

Robbie raised his eyebrows. "What nurse?"

Caden shook his head. "Drunken meanderings. Pay no attention."

As he and Robbie slid into the car, Danny pointed at Caden. "Not that drunk. You need to call her."

Caden turned carefully and started the short walk to his brownstone. The only light in the velvety dark sky came from the streetlights and a few windows of the homes lining the avenue. He made the turn to his street, startled to see the darkness pierced by mini white lights wrapped around every tree. Decorating for the holidays had begun, and it wasn't even Thanksgiving.

He groaned. *Oh man, it's that time of year again.* Three years ago, Caden had been living in the suburbs and had put up outside lights for the first time. He and Mary had decorated the tree he'd picked up from a corner merchant—but before that Christmas season was over, his well-ordered life had fallen apart in a way he never could have foreseen.

I hope nobody realizes how fucked-up I get every December. Maybe this year will be different.

Caden arrived at his home, bounded up the stairs, and punched in the code to unlock the door, but the handle didn't yield. *Damn!* He pressed the numbers again. Same result.

Laughter overtook him. *I should have stopped drinking two beers ago. It's going to be embarrassing if I have to get one of my tenants to let me in.* The door opened on his third attempt. He climbed the stairs to his entry, which thankfully opened on the first try.

Caden went directly to the kitchen, drank a glass of water, refilled the glass, and wandered back to the living room. Danny had to mention calling Quinn. Sure as hell, Robbie would ask about it the next time they were together. Now everyone knew.

Standing in front of the large window, he looked out at the city skyline, took another swallow of water, followed by a deep breath. *I should have left a message when I called two weeks ago. At least now I know why she didn't call me back. I told her I'd be in touch when Claire has the baby, so maybe she wasn't expecting to hear from me yet, anyway.*

Caden had spent most of the past two weeks dwelling on Quinn. Digging out his cell to look at her photo for the thousandth time, he thought about sending a text. *What time is it anyway? Ten thirty. Is she still awake?*

Ah, what the hell!

Before he could stop himself, he let his thumbs tap out the message.

> Remember me? Harvard, spilled chai, pregnant sister?

Caden hit Send and sat looking at his phone. *Delivered* showed on the screen and a few seconds later, *Read*. He took another deep breath and blew it out. *Damn, you'd think I was fifteen years old, asking a girl out for the first time.*

Ellipsis popped up, and his heart jumped. He watched as they disappeared and came back. Finally, a message appeared.

> Quinn: Let me think, kinda short, blond hair?

A smile crossed his face. "She's got a sense of humor," he murmured.

Caden: That must have been Friday's guy. I was Thursday.

Quinn: Oh yeah, blue-eyed doctor sharing his last name with a certain quarterback. I thought you forgot about me.

Caden: No, you're unforgettable.

She sent back a blushing emoji, then a message.

Surprised you aren't out on the town on a Friday night.

Caden: I was at a neighborhood bar with friends earlier.

Quinn: Cheers?

Caden: No, that's not exactly my neighborhood lol.

Quinn: Where is it? Your neighborhood?

Caden: The Back Bay.

Quinn: I love the brownstones there.

Caden: Me too. That's why I bought one.

Quinn: Seriously? You own a brownstone?

Caden: Wanna see?

Quinn: Heck yeah!

He snapped a couple of pictures of the fireplace and the windows and sent them to her. Then he added one taken from the outside a few months earlier.

Quinn: You're not wearing blue.

Caden: No… I don't always wear blue. But how do you know?

Quinn: I can see your reflection in the fireplace pic. You had blue on the three times I saw you in Boston. I figured some woman had probably told you how it enhanced your eyes.

His heart stuttered. He looked at the photo he'd sent. *God, I look like hell.* But it pleased him she had looked so closely at the picture.

Quinn: The brownstone looks exceptional too. Do you live in the whole thing?

Caden: There are two apartments on the first floor. I live on the upper floors.

After a second, he muttered a curse.

I look like hell in that picture. I may have drunk a little too much…

She sent a laughing emoji.

Caden: What do you look like on Friday night?

The selfie she sent showed her dressed in a white tank top under a red flannel shirt and her hair in a messy bun. An orange cat perched on her shoulder.

Caden: That's a big cat! Looks like he's surgically attached to you.

Quinn: He's still recovering from me being gone for a week. He's been staying very close to me.

Caden wished he was the cat.

Caden: You didn't have glasses on in Boston, did you?

Quinn: Nope, contacts. But it's late on a Friday night and I'm studying, so the glasses work.

Caden: Sorry for the distraction.

Quinn: I was ready for a break.

Caden: Are you working this weekend?

Quinn: Tomorrow. I have Sunday off.

Caden: So, you probably want to go to bed?

Quinn: Regretfully, you're correct.

Caden: Got it. Nice talking to you.

Quinn: Yeah, it was.

Caden: Hey, Quinn? Sorry it took me so long to be in touch.

She responded with a smiling emoji. And that brought a smile to his face too.

Caden climbed the stairs to his bedroom and finished a third glass of water, hoping it would stave off a hangover. Stretched out on his bed, he thought about the text conversation, which had gone well, better than he could have expected.

She'd seemed happy to hear from him. Friendly. A little flirty, even.

He thought about the guy they'd had lunch with at Harvard. Sam. He and Quinn had gone to high school together, but he suspected it was more than that. There were daggers in Sam's eyes when Quinn introduced them.

After their lunch, Caden had asked her if there was something going on with Sam because he would not get in the middle of something, no matter how attracted he was to her. She said it was nothing, and she seemed sincere.

I'm going to talk to her again.

> *He wandered through the house, looking for Mary. He heard noises. She must be in the bed-room, getting ready. His shift had ended early, so they'd have some time together before they went out. He opened the bed-*

room door with a smile as he loosened his tie. And there she was on the bed... riding some guy, both moaning in passion.

With his stomach churning, he bellowed, "What the fuck is going on?"

Caden fought his way to consciousness, thrashing his limbs, the sheets entangling him.

It's a dream, a dream. Open your eyes! It's just a dream.

He gasped for air, his heart pounding, as his eyes finally opened. Lying still, he tried to calm his breathing and slow his heart.

Those damn Christmas lights!

Caden climbed out of bed, yanked on his boxers, and made his way to the den, turning on the fireplace before slumping on the leather couch. Brooke had helped him decorate, and she was the one who'd convinced him to make one of the extra rooms into a den, arguing that if he ever had children, it would be easy to turn it back into a bedroom. It was his preferred room in the brownstone, his favorite spot to relax. The walls were a deep cocoa color, and bookshelves lined both sides of the fireplace. Brooke had found an antique music cabinet and turned it into a bar. A bottle of his favorite Irish Whiskey sat on top beside a hammered copper ice bucket. He looked longingly at the bottle, but knew additional alcohol would not chase away the demons haunting him tonight.

Instead, he concentrated on the fire, trying to lose himself in the flames. *Why did the dream have to happen tonight?* It had spoiled the buzz he'd gone to sleep with after talking to Quinn.

He ran his hand through his hair and lay back on the couch, pulling an oatmeal-colored throw over his bare chest. *When the hell will I be done with this?*

After a while, sleep finally caught up with him, and he dozed on the couch until dawn, when he stumbled back to his bed.

Chapter Seven

Football With Ashley

Quinn

ON SUNDAY, QUINN DONNED a vintage Patriots jersey and started making food for the game. She prepared bacon-wrapped smokies and spinach-artichoke dip, both of which she would pop in the oven closer to game time along with loaded Tater Tots.

Ashley was bringing wings from a pub they liked. She was Quinn's only friend who enjoyed football, so they tried to watch the games together whenever their schedules allowed. The snacks and adult beverages were an important part of the games.

My other girlfriends don't know what they're missing.

Caden had texted again on Saturday night, asking if she was going to watch the game. Quinn grinned, thinking about the fun back-and-forth of their texting. *Those messages flowed as naturally as the conversation did on the day we met.*

Caden had been a welcome distraction. Quinn hadn't slept well on Wednesday or Thursday after ending things with Sam. She knew it was the right thing for both of them, but couldn't get the shattered look in Sam's eyes out of her mind. Wracked with guilt, she'd called Angie on Friday night, letting her know what had happened. Angie supported her decision, and that had helped.

But hearing from Caden was a pleasant surprise—one that finally pushed Sam's heartbreak, however temporary she knew it would be, out of her head.

Quinn and Ashley had been on different shifts and hadn't talked since the night they met at the Sidecar. Ashley arrived just before game time, and they spread out the food and popped the tops on a couple of hard ciders before settling down in front of the television.

"How are things on the Sam front.?" Ashley hadn't even taken a sip of her drink before the question Quinn had been dreading spilled out.

"I ended it Wednesday night." Quinn sighed. "He's not over Norah, and I'm not interested in being a distraction." She would not go any deeper into the story, no matter how close a friend Ashley was.

With seconds left in the game, the score was tied when the Patriots' quarterback unleashed a long throw that was caught in the end zone. "Yes!" Ashley punched her fist into the air as Quinn's phone pinged.

> *Caden: What a pass!*

> *Quinn: I know. I was worried.*

> *Caden: Yes, that was too close. Where do you watch the games?*

> *Quinn: I'm at home, watching with one of my girlfriends. How about you?*

He sent a video that panned the frenzied scene at a bar and ended with a shot of him beside a tall blond man who had his arm slung over Caden's shoulder.

Quinn smiled as she watched the brief clip and then looked up, realizing she was ignoring Ashley. "Well, that was rude of me. Sorry." She put her phone down and her eyes met Ashley's questioning gaze. Her cheeks reddened, and she picked up a wing to munch on. When she looked back up, Ashley was still watching her.

"You won't believe this. That was the tall, dark and handsome doctor."

"From Boston?"

Quinn nodded and played the video for her.

"Whoa!" Ashley fanned her face. "You weren't kidding about him being gorgeous. When did this start?"

"Friday night. He admitted he'd been drinking, so I figured maybe it was like a drunk dial." She shrugged her shoulders. "You know? But then he texted last night and now..."

Ashley smiled. "I like this development."

"Yeah, me too."

Caden

Caden waited until the next night to text Quinn again.

> *Caden: Hope you had a good Monday*

> *Quinn: I did. How about you?*

> *Caden: Mondays are always crazy. Were you asleep?*

> *Quinn: No, Max and I are curled up in bed watching TV.*

He opened the picture of Max that Quinn sent and wished it was a picture of her. He also wished he was the one lying on her bed with her instead of the cat.

Since he'd established his pattern—and had been looking forward to it all day—Caden sent a text at ten thirty on Tuesday night.

Caden: Hope you had a good day.

For the first time, nothing came back. The message showed as delivered but not read. Caden sat in the den, nursing a glass of Irish whiskey as he waited for a response. *Maybe she's working or went to bed early.* His moping made him realize how much he looked forward to their nightly exchange of text messages, even though it had only been a few days. Disappointed, he went to bed.

In the morning, his phone showed a message Quinn had sent in the middle of the night.

Quinn: So sorry! Had a hectic day and fell asleep early. Missed talking to you!

Yes! The frown instantly turned upside down. Caden laughed to himself and sent a thumbs-up emoji. His days were too busy to get caught up in texting, and he knew hers probably were as well. Later, though...

When Caden arrived home on Wednesday night, Robbie was sitting on the steps of the brownstone. Six months ago, he had converted the area behind the apartments into a gym, and Robbie worked out with him at least once a week when their schedules allowed.

"Sorry I'm late," Caden said. "I had a crazy day. The workout will feel good tonight."

They rotated through the equipment, and Caden was on the slant board doing crunches when he remembered. "You're still coming for Thanksgiving dinner with the family tomorrow, right? I get off work at three, although if you want to get there earlier, my mother will love it."

Robbie grinned. "I'm sure she would. We're going to volunteer at a shelter Jenny's involved with first, then we'll head to the waterfront after that."

"I told Ma no baby talk."

"I appreciate that." Robbie put down the weights he'd been lifting with a groan. "Hey, did you call that nurse?"

Caden hesitated mid-crunch. "What nurse?"

"The one Danny was talking about Friday night."

Caden rolled off the slant board, sweating heavily, and grabbed a towel. He buried his face in it and, voice muffled, said, "We've been texting." As he wiped the towel down to his shoulders, he finally looked at Robbie, who was grinning at him. Caden sighed. "How much did Danny tell you?"

Robbie shook his head. "Not much. He was rambling like he does whenever he drinks too much. He alternated between the idiocy of the football player and how you'd met a nurse at a conference but were too much of a chickenshit to call her."

"Nice. Shows who my real friends are." Caden couldn't help but smile. "She lives in New Hampshire, near Claire. We're getting to know each other."

Robbie clapped him on the shoulder. "I hope it goes somewhere. You've been alone long enough." He pulled his sweatpants over his shorts. "First hockey game on Saturday. You ready?"

"Yeah." Caden stretched. "It'll feel good to be back on the ice."

They left the gym together, and as Robbie left, he said slyly, "Enjoy your texts."

After a shower, Caden went to the den and considered texting Quinn, but it was early. He enjoyed texting with her just before bed—it relaxed him. He settled in to watch a college basketball game, and just as he picked up his phone, it dinged with a text.

Quinn: Happy Thanksgiving Eve.

Caden: Same to you. Poor us, we don't even get to look forward to the day off tomorrow. I missed talking to you last night.

Quinn: Me too. I think I was asleep before nine. Are all those sisters going to be at dinner?

Caden: No, Claire is staying home because her due date's close. And Cathleen is in North Carolina. My mother is heartbroken that we won't all be there.

Quinn: She likes to keep you close. How did one of you escape?

Caden: Lol. Close doesn't begin to describe my mother. She has no boundaries. Cathleen's always been the most independent of us.

Quinn: Guess I'm lucky. I'm close to my parents, but they aren't overbearing. Hope you have a good day.

Caden: I'm on duty at six, which is good because I'll be out at three and won't hold up Thanksgiving dinner too late.

Quinn: But it means you're on your way to bed.

Caden: Yup, g'night.

Quinn: Night.

He smiled as he set his phone down.

Chapter Eight

Thanksgiving

Quinn

THANKSGIVING NIGHT FOUND QUINN feeling restless. The hospital cafeteria had served a turkey dinner that she enjoyed, but it hardly equaled the meal her mother used to cook. She especially missed her mom's sweet potato casserole with the crunchy praline topping, and no hospital kitchen would ever match the homemade stuffing.

Quinn and Ashley had met at the Sidecar after their shift, staying long enough for two margaritas and a plate of nachos. At home, Quinn gave Max tuna for dinner as a holiday treat. *And I had nachos. What a way to celebrate.* She didn't like to admit it to anyone, but it was rough being alone on Thanksgiving. She'd celebrate with her friends on Saturday, but today loomed long.

The Patriots were playing the late game, at least. Quinn lay down to nap before it began.

Her ringing cell woke her up, and her voice was thick with sleep as she answered it.

"Hey Quinn, were you sleeping? Isn't it only like eight o'clock there?" It was Izzy, calling from her parents' house in Iowa.

"Hi, Izzy." She stretched a little. "You caught me—I was napping before the football game."

"I wanted to wish you a happy Thanksgiving. You told me you'd be alone, and I feel kinda bad about that."

Aw, you thoughtful kid. Quinn was touched. "You're sweet, but I'm fine, really."

"I also have some news. I went to the pool where I trained in high school, and a guy I was on the swim team with was there. We raced, and I beat his ass! And not just by a stroke or two—by half a lap!"

Quinn could hear the excitement in her voice. "That's outstanding! I'm proud of you."

"Thank you! It wiped away those doubts I talked to you about last week. It was all in the turns, and I owe my improvement to you."

"I'm glad I could help, but you're the one who put the work in."

"What about you? How did it work out with the hard thing you needed to do?"

Quinn should have expected that question. Izzy didn't have a reserved bone in her body. "It went about like I thought it would."

"You broke the fast, so now you need to get right back on that horse," Izzy advised. "There must be a doctor in your hospital who'd be willing to scratch your itch."

Quinn laughed. "You've got a lot of metaphors going on there. And who said I had an itch?"

By then, Izzy was laughing too. "It's the creative-writing course I'm taking. But you know what I mean."

Quinn thought about Caden. "I promise you this. If I go on a date, you'll be the first to know."

The game was in the third quarter and Quinn was halfway through her second glass of wine when her cell rang again. *Who in the world would call me at ten thirty?* She looked at the caller ID, and her stomach tingled in an unfamiliar way as she answered.

"Hello?"

"Hi." Caden's voice was soft and sexy, and the tingling in Quinn's stomach intensified. "I wanted to hear your voice. Is this okay?"

"Of course." She hoped her voice sounded normal. "How was your Thanksgiving?"

"Only two turkey-carving incidents while I was working. That was a good thing." She could hear the smile in his voice. "My mom cooked a totally traditional dinner, and I ate way too much. Now I'm happy to be home in comfortable clothes, drinking a beer and talking to you."

"I had a turkey dinner at work, and I'll toast your beer with my glass of wine. I talked to my parents, and they went to a big gathering at one of their neighbors. Mom said it was very Southern with a bit of religion thrown in, like they said grace before dinner." *Oh hell, that was probably the wrong thing to say.* "You must be religious, Irish Catholic, right? Is grace a thing?"

Caden chuckled. "What gave it away, the last name or the five kids?"

"Well, I have to say, I don't know any families with five kids." *Shit.* "Oh. I don't mean to offend. I have nothing against Catholics, or religion, or grace..."

"Quinn, it's okay." His tone was still warm. "No offense taken. We don't say grace. I gather you are not Catholic."

"No. I'm a druid—more spiritual than religious. Do you go to church?"

"Not really. I went until confirmation and then I stopped." There was a pause, then Caden continued, "I'm sorry you didn't have anyone to celebrate with."

His voice was like a soft caress, and Quinn's breath caught. "I don't tell many people, but I was a little lonely. Hearing from you this way is nice." She fought to get her emotions under control. "Are you working all weekend?"

"I have Saturday off. I play ice hockey with my buddies, and we have our first game that day."

"You skate? Did you play hockey in high school? College?"

"I played youth hockey and high school hockey. Nowhere near good enough to play in college. How about you? Are you a skater?"

"Only if I have a milk crate to hang on to."

Caden chuckled. "We'll have to fix that. I'll teach you how to skate. Do you do any sports?"

"I swim and ski." She hesitated, then told him about Izzy and how she'd called. Caden listened attentively, and she enjoyed his reactions.

After they said goodbye, Quinn finished her wine and thought about Caden's deep voice. It had gone from matter of fact when he was talking about dinner with his family or hockey with his friends to warm and tender when he spoke to her more personally.

The butterflies returned to her stomach.

Caden

On the walk home from O'Malley's on Friday night, the Christmas lights still annoyed Caden. He knew more and more lights would appear as the season progressed. At least he hadn't had the dream again. Yet. *January can't get here soon enough.*

Caden settled in the den, the fireplace casting a warm glow as he relaxed with a shot of Irish whiskey. He was looking forward to getting back on the ice with Danny, Robbie, and the rest of their team. He thought about Quinn telling him she didn't know how to skate. Teaching her would be fun.

He pictured holding her hands to pull her around the rink, and it stirred long-dormant feelings. *Should I buy her a pair of skates? No, that's probably coming on a little strong. Plus, I have no idea what size she wears.*

Their conversation at ten thirty was brief, but Quinn promised to call him the next night when she was home after dinner with her friends.

Caden called his sister Claire on Saturday morning. "That baby ready to be born?"

"Apparently not, although I am more than ready for him to vacate his cushy digs." Claire told him about her various physical issues related to the pregnancy, and he listened as a dutiful brother. After giving her plenty of time to complain, he broached the subject he had at least partially called for.

"I need to discuss something with you. I went to a conference a few weeks ago and met a nurse who works at Dartmouth."

"And you want me to use my super-sleuthing skills to check her out? Get her number for you?"

"No, she gave me her number the day we met. We've been talking, and I'm planning to see her when I come up." He paused. "I need you to run interference with Mom. Fend off her questions."

Claire sighed. "I will have just pushed a baby out of my body, and you want me to keep Mom from finding out about your love life?" But she said it with a laugh.

Caden grinned. He knew she'd help him. "Thanks, Claire."

"Are you still planning to stay in the guesthouse? Or will you stay with her?"

"Yeah, yeah, I'll be at the guesthouse. I don't want to rush things." Although he'd thought about it. "That's why I don't want Mom to know and ask a million questions. I'm not sure where it's going, but I like her more than I've liked anyone in a long time."

At midafternoon, Caden headed to the ice rink for the hockey game. He and his teammates played hard for two hours, then hit O'Malley's.

The pub was busier than it had been Friday night, and Caden enjoyed sharing food and laughs with Danny and Robbie as they all drank and watched football. His phone vibrated, and he fished it out, finding a picture of a group of people around a table laden with food. Quinn was on the left side with a big grin on her face.

Robbie was right at Caden's shoulder, and he saw the pic before Caden could hide it. He nudged Caden. "Is one of them the nurse?"

Caden grinned, but ignored the question. He wasn't ready to talk about Quinn.

He was sitting in the den when his phone pinged. It was a picture of Quinn in the same black top she had on in the group pic, and Max was in her arms.

Quinn: I'm home. Are you?

Caden: I am.

His phone rang a few seconds later, and his heart beat a little faster. "Hi. How was the party?"

"It was fun, but honestly, now I'm exhausted." She sounded it. "I'm an introvert, and as much as I love spending time with my friends, that many people are overwhelming. How did you spend the day, other than playing hockey?"

"I called Claire this morning to see how she's doing and if there's any sign of this baby coming soon." He stopped.

"And..."

"She's kinda grumpy. Ready for the baby to be born." His voice softened. "I told her about you."

"What about me?"

"That I am going to spend some time with you while I'm up there, and I'm hoping she'll deflect questions from my mom about where I am. Hope you don't mind." He held his breath.

"I don't mind. I've told one of my friends about you. Is your whole family coming up when the baby is born? All the other sisters?"

"No, only me, initially." Caden chuckled in a rush of relief. "Well, my parents, of course, but of the siblings, I get to be first."

"Because of the boy thing?"

"More because Claire and I are the closest. We're only eleven months apart. The rest of the girls are significantly younger. There's fifteen years between my youngest sister and me."

"Your parents figured out what was causing those babies after the first two, huh?" Quinn teased.

"Oh yeah. And of course, they only had sex five times."

Quinn laughed. "And my poor parents only did it once. There was a time I actually believed that."

"My dad made sure I knew where babies came from. It was probably the most awkward experience of my life. How'd you figure it out?"

"I had the same boyfriend my last two years of high school, and my mom was very much a realist about the fact we would likely have sex, so she was extremely open with me. There was a lot of emphasis on making planned decisions, not getting swept up in a moment's passion."

He was glad she had that kind of guidance. "Did you heed that?"

Quinn's voice was measured when she answered. "We were responsible. How about you?"

"Not sure *responsible* is the right word for teenage me." Caden laughed, a little embarrassed.

"A player, huh?"

"Something like that. I've reformed, though." Had he ever.

"I went through a wild phase a few years ago, and I guess you could say I've reformed as well. I haven't dated since I've been at Dartmouth."

Interesting. "But you'll go out with me?"

"I'm looking forward to going out with you." Quinn's voice was soft and sexy.

His answering rush of desire deepened his own voice. "Me too." Caden wondered if she could hear it.

She must have, because she said, "Your sister needs to have that baby soon."

He grinned. "I agree."

After the call ended, Caden decided he would make the trip to New Hampshire the next weekend, regardless of whether the baby had been born.

Should I surprise her? No, my experiences with surprises are not the best. He would tell her later in the week.

Chapter Nine

Quinn Sends A Bathing Suit Pic

Caden

CADEN WAS ON HIS tenth patient Sunday morning when his watch vibrated. Glancing at it, he saw a picture of an indoor pool, and he was sure Quinn sent it to show him she had gone swimming before work. His phone was in his pocket, and he didn't have one free second to take it out, so the picture would have to wait until his lunch break.

The morning went by in a flash, and an intern joined Caden on the walk to the cafeteria. While they were waiting in line,

Caden pulled out his cell, eager to see the picture Quinn had sent.

His breath caught as he saw that there were two pictures, and the second one was of her in a red bathing suit.

The intern standing behind him saw the picture as well. "Hey, boss, who's the babe?"

Caden swiped the phone to make the image disappear and ignored the question. He knew it wouldn't get asked again, but he suspected the picture wouldn't stay a secret. Gossip ran rampant in the ED. Caden had a strong, professional relationship with his colleagues, but he shared little about his personal life for a reason. There had been enough turnover in the department that few of his current co-workers knew what he had gone through nearly three years earlier. He didn't know if he'd ever be as open about his life as he had been in his early to mid-twenties. It's too hard when circumstances change.

Stopping at his locker on the way back to the ED—and thankfully the room was empty—Caden studied the picture again, this time without interruption. God, she was gorgeous, all soft curves, beautiful skin, and long, dark hair. Looking at the picture in the cafeteria had aroused him, and his reaction was the same now.

He sent the emoji with blushing cheeks and hearts for eyes.

Quinn

As Quinn cooked her dinner, she thought about how she'd taken advantage of her late shift to stop at the pool on her way to the hospital. Without thinking, she had snapped a pic of the pool and a selfie and sent them both to Caden.

She was surprised during her break to see Caden had replied with a cute emoji. It made her warm inside to know he liked the picture.

She was curled up in bed when her cell rang.

Caden's first words were "My God, Quinn, do you know what your picture did to me?"

With a smile on her face that she hoped came through in her voice, Quinn said, "You liked it?"

"Oh man, I was instantly turned on."

Her smile changed to laughter. "Thanks for not sending me a picture of that."

Caden joined in. "Well, I was in the cafeteria line. It might have been a little awkward."

"Oops. I thought you wouldn't see it till the end of the day."

"You expected me to wait until the end of the day? Come on. I knew there was a message from you—I couldn't hold off. I looked at it as soon as I had a free minute. But wait, have you gotten pictures of..."

"Oh yeah. Dating apps. You're having a friendly conversation with someone you've swiped on, and the next thing you know, you're looking at... well, you know."

Caden scoffed. "Kinda crude."

"Ya think?"

"You've never sent boob shots?"

Quinn rolled her eyes, indignant. "Not to someone I'd just started talking to! Have you *gotten* boob shots?"

"Yup, guys aren't the only ones who can be crude."

"I see how it is," Quinn teased. "You have an album on your cell filled with boob shots, and you pull them up whenever you're bored."

"No!"

Quinn could hear the horror in his voice. "I'm kidding." She smiled. "But you've gone the dating-app route?"

"I gave it a shot, but it wasn't what I was looking for."

Tell me about it. "Yeah, I finally realized people on dating apps are only looking for hookups, and I gave all that up."

"You're not looking for a hookup?" Caden's voice had changed to that soft tone he had used Thanksgiving night. The one Quinn found so sexy.

She matched his softness. "Truthfully, I didn't think I was looking for anything."

"But if it lands in your lap?"

"I'll see where it goes."

"Same for me." She could hear him smiling. "You said last night you haven't dated since you've been at Dartmouth, so two years?"

"Probably a little longer." *Sam and I never went on a date, so technically, I'm not lying.* She hoped Sam was okay. *Dammit, I wish that had never happened.*

"It's been more than a year for me," Caden admitted.

Quinn's stomach started fluttering, and her voice caught as she said, "People always say something will come along when you're not looking for it."

"People may be right," he murmured.

"Might be."

They said goodbye, but just before he hung up, Caden said, "Quinn, you can send me a bathing suit picture anytime you want."

After she ended the call, the fluttering in Quinn's stomach lasted for several minutes. *I've got it bad.*

Her thoughts drifted to Sam. *That was all nostalgia and libido. I can't deny how hot the sex was in Boston, but it didn't carry back here.* She hoped again that he was okay. His heartbreak had been obvious, although she suspected some of that was still for Norah. *Eventually we'll be able to be friends, and we'll be better off that way.*

She snuggled deeper under the covers. *But Caden—this differs from anything I've felt before.*

On Monday night, Quinn was able to tell Caden she'd finished her schoolwork for the semester. She was looking forward to her day off.

The next morning, Quinn stretched as she woke up and smiled to herself. *Nothing to do today—how delicious is that?* At the pool, she snapped a selfie in her black one-piece and sent it to Caden with a heart emoji. Another race with Izzy and a long shower invigorated her, and afterward, she spent a couple of hours shopping, feeling in control of her life for the first time in weeks.

Back home, she poured a glass of wine, lit a fire, and sat down to relax. Thoughts of Caden filled every corner of her mind. He would come to Hanover that weekend—she was sure of it. Her mind explored the possibilities. *We'll go out to dinner as he promised, and what then?* She loved the getting-to-know-you dance they'd been doing, and she wanted to spend time with him, but she didn't want to rush into having sex.

Caden's first words to her that night were "I can't decide which I like better, the black suit or the red one. Today's pic had the same effect as Sunday's. Do I have more colors to look forward to?"

Quinn snickered. "Possibly. I have a bit of a shopping obsession."

He sighed, sounding happy. "Something to look forward to. I need that."

The last part came out in a defeated tone Quinn hadn't heard before. "Are you okay?"

Another less-happy sigh. "I'm not good company tonight. I've had a few beers, and I need to go to sleep, but I couldn't miss touching base with you."

Quinn hesitated. This was a different side of him. *Should I ask what happened? Are we close enough for that?* She wasn't sure, but she had to offer something. "Do you want to talk about it?"

"I lost an eight-year-old boy this afternoon." His voice cracked. "It was a terrible car accident. His mother and sister are in the ICU. I had to tell the dad just before my day ended."

"Oh, Caden, that must have been rough."

"Yeah." She could feel his grief. "It hits hard anytime a patient doesn't make it, but when it's a kid..."

There was a long pause, and Quinn sensed he was trying to pull himself together. She gave him time.

After a few moments, he spoke again, sounding a little more normal. "So, I'm going to go to bed, and when I call you tomorrow, I'll be back to my sparkling self."

She wished she could hug him. "I'll be happy to hear from you, even if you aren't."

"Your picture was the high point of my day." His voice was soft, with a tinge of sadness still in it.

Caden

Caden took a deep breath before he called Quinn on Wednesday night. *I shouldn't have called last night. I shouldn't have dumped that on her.*

Quinn answered before Caden even heard it ring.

"Hey." Her voice was hushed, and he suspected she wasn't sure what his mood would be.

"Hey yourself." He hoped Quinn could feel his excitement. "Claire's in labor. My parents arrived a couple of hours ago, and my mom has been updating me on her progress. The last message said she was nine centimeters dilated."

He heard Quinn clap her hands. "That's exciting!"

"I know. And not just because of the baby. I'll finally get to make good on my dinner invitation from so many weeks ago. Are you free on Friday?"

"Hmm. Let me check my calendar."

Caden recognized her teasing tone, so he waited, smiling.

"Well," she said, "I had planned to trim Max's nails, but he won't mind if I put it off." She tried, unsuccessfully, to hide her laughter.

"Will you do me the honor of joining me for dinner?"

"So formal, Dr. Brady. It will be my pleasure to join you."

"I was hoping you'd say that." His voice softened. "I was coming up this weekend if Claire had the baby or not because I can't wait any longer to see you again."

"I'm looking forward to seeing you again, too." That new, sensual tone had the same effect as the bathing suit pictures. But just as quickly, she was back to being playful. "I have to ask you something. Did they teach you in med school how to switch your voice from all business to soft and sexy? Because that soft voice is making me want to crawl through the phone to get at you."

Chuckling, Caden said, "Your voice can be very sexy, and I'd be in heaven if you could come through the phone."

"That voice might make me... come over the phone."

He mock-gasped. "Quinn Michaels, you have a dirty mind."

"You said it first! I said crawl."

Caden collapsed into laughter. "You're killing me. I can't wait until Friday."

The next morning, Caden called Quinn, hoping to catch her before she left for work.

"Good morning, Caden," she said.

He grinned. "That's Uncle Caden."

"Congratulations! Give me the details."

"Rory James, born at one twenty-five this morning. Eight pounds, one ounce, twenty inches long. Apgar of ten."

"Of course it's ten. He's your nephew!"

He snickered. "Mom didn't really tell me the Apgar, but you're right. He's my nephew—it must be a ten."

She laughed. "Are you at work?"

"Yeah, I had a minute, and I wanted to call before you left for the day. I know you must be getting out the door, so I'll talk to you tonight."

That night, Caden was frazzled, trying to pack. Normally, everything he'd need for a weekend could fit in a backpack, but he felt like more than jeans and T-shirts were called for. He and Quinn were going to Molly's for dinner. It had great reviews, and he thought about taking a blazer before deciding it would be too much. Knowing the north country was more relaxed, he decided on a sweater and good jeans.

More stylish dinner wear could wait for Quinn's visits to Boston. *I can't wait to show her my favorite places.*

What else would he need to take? Caden hoped to see Quinn for more than Friday night, but wasn't sure what they would do on Saturday. *Ice skating?* Maybe. He would throw his skates in the car. *Swimming?* That was possible. Swim trunks went in his bag. It had been a long time since he was so nervous in anticipation of a date.

He texted Claire and asked her to call if she wasn't sleeping. His phone rang a few seconds later.

"Hello," Claire said softly when he picked up.

"Congratulations! Can't wait to meet him."

"Oh, Cade, I fell instantly in love. He's got a headful of dark hair like all of us did. And his eyes are blue. James is hoping they stay that color. I've counted his little fingers and toes. He's just perfect."

"I'm so happy for you, Claire. Was labor as bad as you feared?"

"Oh, yeah, but totally worth it. I won't be having five like Mom did, but I'll definitely do it again." She paused. "What time do you plan to get here tomorrow? And have you made plans with your nurse?"

"I should be there between ten and eleven. I made a reservation for dinner at Molly's."

"Good choice. Any other plans?"

"Nothing beyond that."

He could hear soft baby cries in the background.

"I need to go," Claire said. "See you tomorrow."

He thought for a few minutes about how happy Claire sounded, then he called Quinn.

"Hi, Uncle Caden."

He could hear a smile in her voice. "Hi, that feels weird. Being referred to as 'uncle.'"

"Have you talked to your sister?"

"I just did. She's in love. I'm happy for her and James. I'm very excited to meet my nephew."

"You like babies." It was more a statement than a question.

Caden's voice went soft. "I do. Did I tell you I delivered one, the day after we met?"

"No! That's a little out of the ordinary for you, isn't it?"

"It sure was. How about you? Are you a fan of wee humans?"

Quinn hesitated. "I like babies," she said. "Although, to be honest, I don't have a lot of experience."

"My experience started early with three younger sisters." Man, he wished he could be there with her already. "I'm looking forward to seeing you. I made a reservation at Molly's for seven tomorrow night. Does that work for you?"

"Yes. I've been there once. It was delicious. And seven works well for me."

He breathed a little sigh of relief. "I'll talk to you after I see Claire. See you tomorrow." He paused, then grinned. "I enjoy being able to say that."

"I enjoy hearing that. And Caden?" Her voice lowered a little. "I can't wait to see you."

Chapter Ten

The First Date

Quinn

ON FRIDAY, QUINN WAS changing an IV for a patient who had been on the ward for many weeks and was one of her favorites when a nurse popped into the room.

"Quinny," she announced, "there's someone at the station looking for you."

Quinn nodded, focusing. "Okay, I'll be about five minutes."

"A very handsome guy."

Caden? "Okay, I'll be about four minutes and fifty seconds."

It had to be him. *Oh man, this is going to lead to an avalanche of gossip, but...* Her stomach fluttered the same way it did when she talked to Caden on the phone. She'd worn her favorite royal-blue scrub top, so she knew she looked good, but it didn't quiet the nerves she felt about seeing him in person.

Quinn finished with her patient and walked back to the nurse's station. Coming around the corner, she caught her breath when she saw him. He had on a black half-zip and well-fitting jeans. The smile that had simmered below the surface since she'd known he was there bloomed wide across her face. The nurses at the station were trying to look busy, but it was obvious they were watching.

She walked up to Caden and stuck out her hand, hoping he would follow her lead. "Dr. Brady, how nice to see you again after the conference. Did your sister have her baby?"

He grasped her hand in a brief, businesslike shake. "Yes. I thought since I was in town, I'd stop and say hello."

Quinn gave him a very subtle nod. "Let me show you around." She started to lead Caden away, but stopped, turning back to face her colleagues. "You can all go back to work now." She waved her hand to shoo them away and continued toward the hallway.

Caden followed. "I wanted to hug you, but I wasn't sure how you'd feel about that," he murmured when they were a safe distance away.

"I would have loved it, but God, I'd never hear the end of it." She stopped in front of a large bank of windows and turned to face him. "Have you been to see Claire?"

"Yes, and they are getting ready to release her, so I was in the way. I figured I'd come say hi to you, then head over to her house for the afternoon."

He looked out the window at the surrounding hillside, which was forested with both hardwood and softwood trees. "This view is beautiful. It must be nice to work in this environment."

Quinn nodded. "It is." She pointed out the recreation path that went around the hospital and through the woods. "I usually walk there at the end of my shift."

Caden took out his phone and showed her a picture of him holding Rory.

"Oh, just seeing you isn't enough. You show me a picture of you holding a baby, the way to every woman's heart!" She grinned up at him. He was even better looking than she remembered, with his hair slightly longer and curling over his ears.

He extended his hand out to brush a loose piece of hair off her face. "I don't care about every woman," he said, voice soft. When his fingers grazed her skin, a jolt of electricity went through her. "I shouldn't keep you from your work, but I need to know where to pick you up."

Quinn gave him her address, then bid him goodbye and watched him walk back down the hall. *Looking good from all angles, Dr. Brady.*

Questioning eyes met her at the nurse's station, and she held up a hand. "We sat together one day at the conference. He mentioned his sister and said he would stop by to say hello when he came to visit. That's it."

The nurses all grinned at her.

One, who had a reputation for dating a different doctor every month, said, "Well, if you're not interested in him, I sure could be. Do you have his phone number?"

Quinn frowned and shook her head. "Sorry, but no, I don't." She went to check on a patient and laughed to herself. *I wouldn't give you his number if my life depended on it.*

The afternoon crawled by, and when her shift finally ended, Quinn didn't linger. Once home, she showered and then tried on and rejected several tops, finally deciding on a purple V-neck sweater, black leggings, and boots. She left her hair down and wore silver earrings with a silver necklace.

Only a few minutes now. Quinn watched out the window, taking deep breaths to calm herself. Caden arrived promptly at six thirty. She walked out to him as he was approaching her door, and his open arms enveloped her.

"Even with coats on, this feels as good as I imagined it would," he murmured into her hair.

She agreed, her head settled on his chest.

When they walked to his car, a midnight-blue BMW sports car, he opened the door for her.

"Nice car."

"Thanks. What do you drive?"

"A Subaru Outback. It's kind of the unofficial car of Vermont, and I still regard myself as a Vermonter."

The host led them to a table next to the fireplace. As Caden helped her take off her coat, his hand brushed against her neck, and butterflies invaded her stomach. Quinn had seldom had someone open her car door or help with her coat. Caden was truly a different kind of guy than she was accustomed to.

Caden wore a gray shirt with a blue sweater, those jeans that fit so well, and boots. Not steel-toed work boots or sneakers, like most of the men she knew, but nice, stylish boots.

They ordered drinks, white wine for Quinn, and a craft beer for Caden.

"I think you had that sweater on the night we saw each other in the hotel bar. You look beautiful."

She knew she was blushing. "Good memory. You're wearing blue—trying to make me notice your eyes?"

"Could be. Is it working?"

"Those eyes are hard to ignore."

He grinned and looked at the menu. "What looks good to you?"

"I'm going to have the salmon. How about you?"

"Steak, probably the filet. I'm a total carnivore."

"I like a good steak too, but salmon's my favorite."

He nodded. "I'm glad you ordered more than a salad."

Quinn laughed. "Oh, I like to eat."

"Did I embarrass you by stopping at the hospital?"

"My colleagues were curious. I've never had a man stop by before. One of them wanted your number." She grinned at him.

He grinned back. "And did you give it to her?"

"Hell no!"

After they ordered, they chatted easily, and he asked how long she'd lived in the town house.

"I bought it about a month after I started at the hospital. I stayed at my parents' condo up north while I looked for something here." She gestured at him. "How long have you been in the Back Bay? I still can't believe I know someone who lives in one of those brownstones."

"Two and a half years. I lived farther out before. It took me more than an hour to get to work on the T back then. Now I can walk it in fifteen minutes."

Their food came, and while they were eating, Caden asked, "Hey, how was your dinner in Boston the night we met? You went to Carmelina's, didn't you?"

Quinn remembered what happened with Sam after dinner and dipped her head as her cheeks warmed. "It was good."

His expression was quizzical. "You're blushing."

Thinking quickly, she told him about falling asleep in the Uber and the driver calling her Sleeping Beauty. It was the truth. Part of it.

"Ah, so you were Aurora." He smiled, and then the smile faded. "Did it take a kiss from a handsome prince to wake you up?"

She laughed, hoping it didn't sound too self-conscious. "No. A simple tap on the shoulder did the trick."

"Have you and Sam stayed in touch since then?"

She felt her face redden even more. *This is dangerous territory.*

After a pause, he continued, "You mentioned you would probably not see him for another ten years. I wondered about the significance of ten years. Is it like a reunion thing?"

Quinn had made a promise to herself that in her next relationship, she would be honest and direct. No more hiding things or telling the guy what he wanted to hear. But she could not tell him about trying to rekindle things with Sam. Not on their first date.

She took a deep breath. "We dated in high school and broke up soon after I started college. I hadn't seen him in ten years, didn't expect to run into him, and don't expect to see him for another ten years." She looked directly at Caden, figuring he was probably thinking about their conversation about their first times having sex.

He raised his eyebrows as he said, "So..."

Bingo. Quinn didn't let him finish the question. "Yes."

Looking down at her plate, she stabbed the last bite of the salmon.

When she lifted her head again, he was gazing at her, his blue eyes soft. "Do you want to share a brownie sundae for dessert?"

She nodded, relaxing a little, and he ordered the sundae with two spoons. The server placed it in the middle of the table, and Caden's eyes twinkled as he dug into the whipped cream first and held out his spoon to feed it to her.

She swallowed and sighed. "That's delicious." Mimicking his motions, she filled her spoon with ice cream covered in fudge sauce and lifted it to his mouth.

"Mmm, it is."

Feeding each other took away more of Quinn's tension. They polished off the sundae, their spoons battling for the last bite. When the server came back to ask if they wanted coffee or anything else, Quinn looked at Caden. "We can go back to my place for a nightcap."

"I'd like that." Caden helped her with her coat and took her hand as they walked to his car. He paused before opening the door, and for a breathless moment, she thought he would kiss her.

Back at the townhouse, Quinn unlocked the door. "My town house is totally generic. There were probably thousands like it built in the nineties."

"But it's yours. That's what matters."

When they stepped inside, he helped her with her coat again.

She smiled at him. "I rarely have a man open the car door for me or help me with my coat. I could get used to it."

Caden dipped his head. "My grandfather and my dad were sticklers for manners, and it stayed with me."

"What do you want to drink?" Quinn asked, leading him to the living room. "I don't have beer, but I have ciders and wine, and I make a mean Irish coffee."

"With Jameson?"

She raised her eyebrows. "Is there any other Irish whiskey?"

He grinned. "You have good taste. I'll try your coffee."

Quinn handed him her phone and pointed out the docking station. "There's a bunch of playlists. See if you can find one you like." She moved to the kitchen, leaving him to look around. "The fireplace is ready to be lit. Can you do that too?"

While lighting the fire, he called out, "Hey, where's Max? I thought I'd get to meet him."

"He's very shy," she called back. "I'm sure he's hiding upstairs."

While the coffee was brewing, Quinn peeked around the corner and saw Caden looking at her books. She knew he also noticed her framed mountaintop photos when he asked, "You like to hike?"

She came back into the living room, carrying two mugs. "Yes, I enjoy hiking. I love getting to the top of mountains and seeing a magnificent view. I like a view no matter where I am. My room was on the twenty-fifth floor in Boston, and I spent time every day looking out at the city."

"Where are the pictures from?"

"Mount Hood, a few peaks in Washington and Colorado, and Mount Pisgah in Vermont." She handed him a mug and led him to the couch in front of the fireplace, where a roaring fire crackled. "Nice job on the fire. And the music."

"It took some genuine talent." He chuckled playfully. "You had both all set to go. Your playlists are very eclectic." He had chosen soft jazz.

"Different phases, I guess. Sometimes I go back and listen to old ones and feel nostalgic, and sometimes I wonder what I was thinking."

They sipped from their mugs, letting the whiskey warm their insides.

"You weren't kidding," he mused. "This is a killer Irish coffee."

After another sip, Caden put his mug down and reached for hers, setting it on the table next to his. His arms extended, pulling her toward him. She leaned in to meet him.

Their kiss started out soft and tentative, but it quickly intensified. Quinn felt the kiss deep in her core. She opened her mouth, and their tongues tangled. Sighing, she melted toward him. They continued to explore each other for endless minutes.

Caden pulled back, loosening his hold. "I think I've wanted to do that since I saw you drop your chai in Cambridge. And it was better than I imagined."

Quinn nodded, settling back. "For me too."

Caden picked up his mug and took another sip. "I'm sorry if I made you uncomfortable back there in the restaurant by asking about Sam."

Before she could respond, Max jumped into Caden's lap and nuzzled his chest.

"Well, hi, Max. How are you, big boy? Do I meet with your approval?" Caden petted the cat, and Max continued making himself comfortable in Caden's lap. His paws reached up, first to Caden's chest and then his neck. Caden looked at Quinn with bewilderment in his eyes. "Is he hugging me?"

Quinn shook her head. "He literally never does this. I have friends who have been here several times, and they've never even seen him."

Max tilted his head and jumped from Caden to Quinn, purring loudly.

"About Sam," she began, rubbing Max's head. "Asking was fine. You could tell we were more than acquaintances. He's not a part of my life now."

"I'm glad to hear that." Gently, Caden picked up Max and lowered him to the floor. "Sorry, buddy, but you're in the way."

Caden embraced her again, seeking her lips. Her tongue went into his mouth to explore, and Caden nibbled on her bottom lip. She melted against him, loving the feel of his hands on her back.

Eventually, Caden nudged her down onto the couch cushions and lowered himself onto her. At the pressure of his body against hers, her center throbbed. Sighing softly, she slid her arms around his back, gripping his muscles. His hand slid under her sweater, stroking her skin.

But when his fingers touched her breast, Quinn froze, remembering her last morning with Sam.

Slowly, Caden removed his hand and sat up. She could see the question in his eyes before she pulled herself upright.

"What's wrong?" he asked.

"I'm sorry, I... can we slow it down? It's not that I'm not into you, because I definitely am. It's just... I've had enough casual sex to last a lifetime, and I'm not looking for that." She put her hands over her face.

Caden took her hands in his, gently lifting them away from her face. "Casual isn't what I'm looking for either. I got carried away. I'm sorry." He kissed her again, lightly this time. "For the record, I'm definitely into you, too." His arms went around her back, and he simply held her. Quinn relaxed into him, relishing his warmth and the beating of his heart.

When he let her go, she lifted her hand to his cheek. "I want to get to know you better."

"I want that too," he said, smiling. "Can we do something tomorrow?"

"I'd like that. Do you want to go hiking?"

"Sure. It's not too cold yet."

"I haven't hiked around here." Quinn thought for a minute. "I usually look for mountains to conquer, but I think the Appalachian Trail is nearby."

Caden picked up his phone, and together they searched for a map. They figured out where to go and agreed to start early in the afternoon, so they would have about three hours before dark. With plans for the next day settled, they returned to kissing, more gently than before.

"So, this is part of getting to know each other?" Quinn murmured.

"Yes," Caden said as he nuzzled her neck. "This is absolutely part of it."

The make-out session continued until Quinn failed to suppress a yawn.

Caden pulled back. "You must be tired. You worked all day."

"Yeah, a little."

He stood to go but drew her into a hug first, saying, "I enjoyed tonight."

"So did I." Quinn hugged him back, then walked him to the door, where he kissed her one last time.

Quinn walked slowly, contentedly, to her room, remembering Caden's kisses. She took off her clothes and snuggled into bed with Max, thinking about the evening.

It had lived up to all her expectations. The conversation flowed effortlessly. His manners and kindness blew her away, and his kisses traveled all the way to her toes.

Why the hell did I have to think about Sam in the middle of things? I hope I didn't blow it by asking him to slow it down.

When her phone rang, she smiled and answered.

"I really enjoyed tonight." Caden's voice was soft.

"So did I, but... do you think I'm weird for wanting to wait?"

"No. I like how you aren't afraid to say what you want. Are you in bed?"

Quinn matched his hushed voice. "Yes."

"With Max?"

"Yes."

He sighed. "Lucky cat. What do you wear to bed?"

"Use your imagination."

Caden sighed again. "My imagination is creating a very hot picture."

"How about you?" she teased. "What do you wear to bed?"

"The suit I was born in." He chuckled.

"That's a hot picture too." Quinn paused. *Say what you want.* In a matter-of-fact voice, she asked, "Do you want to stay for dinner after the hike tomorrow, then watch a movie?

"I'd like that. See you tomorrow."

She smiled.

Chapter Eleven

Getting To Know You

Caden

As soon as Caden's eyes opened, Quinn popped into his mind. At first, thinking about the night before was pleasant, then he was appalled to remember letting himself get carried away.

I hope I didn't fuck things up, because she was everything I thought she would be.

He reluctantly crawled out of the guesthouse's comfortable bed. Upon picking up his phone, he saw texts from Claire letting him know their mother had asked where he was the night before, but she had covered for him by inventing a friendly dinner with a college classmate named Michael. But she wasn't sure their mother bought the story.

When Caden walked into the main house, his mother was in the kitchen, holding Rory and making breakfast. Reaching out, he took Rory from her and cooed to him before asking his mom, "Is Claire sleeping?"

"I hope so. She just finished nursing, so I took the baby to let her sleep." She opened the oven to take out the bacon. "You had dinner with a college friend last night? I don't remember you knowing anyone up this way."

Caden shrugged. "You don't know all my friends."

"No?"

"Nope. You got some breakfast there for me?"

Mom took Rory as Caden filled a plate with pancakes and bacon.

"I want that baby back after I eat," Caden said, his mouth full. "You're going to have all week with him."

Laughing, she joined him at the table. They both looked up as Claire's husband, James, trudged into the kitchen, looking like he hadn't slept at all.

Caden waved sympathetically. "Rough night?"

James nodded. "Rory's in the room with me and Claire. I didn't realize how many little noises a baby could make. I don't think either of us slept more than a couple of hours." Caden watched him look lovingly at the baby in his mother-in-law's arms. "But he is cute, isn't he?"

After breakfast, Caden spent the rest of the morning holding Rory and visiting with his parents while Claire and James slept. He relished the weight and warmth of the baby in his arms. *Yup, I'm ready for this, and if things had gone differently three years ago, I'd be holding my own child.*

He stopped that train of thought. *Don't go there. You've taken a step toward the future. Stay focused on that.*

Claire and James wandered into the living room shortly before noon, looking a little more rested.

Mom looked at him. "Cade, we're going to get Chinese takeout for either lunch or dinner. Do you have a preference?"

"I won't be here for dinner, and I actually need to head out soon. Don't worry about me."

Rory stirred in his arms and began to fret. Claire took him, then settled in a chair to nurse.

Caden stood and whispered in Claire's ear, "You're beautiful. I'm elated for you." He hugged his mom. "I'll see you all in the morning."

Mom raised her eyebrows. "Where are you going? To see your friend Michael again?"

"Tomorrow, Ma. I'll see you tomorrow."

Caden walked toward the door and stopped. "Hey, James, come here." He motioned toward the kitchen. James joined him there. "Where's there a florist around here?"

"A florist?" Despite Caden's effort to keep his voice low, his mother had heard him. "Who are you taking flowers to?"

Caden sighed and looked at James. "See what it was like growing up with that hearing? None of us got away with anything."

James laughed and gave him the name of a local florist, adding in a near-whisper, "Claire has told me how she always got caught if she tried to sneak out."

On his way to Quinn's, Caden stopped at the shop James recommended, buying an arrangement with white roses, red carnations, and holly. He knocked promptly at one o'clock and was pleased by the smile on Quinn's face when she opened the door.

"Oh my." Quinn reached for the flowers and breathed deeply. "Wow."

Caden followed her to the dining table, where she placed the arrangement. "Glad you like," he said as he grasped her wrist, pulling her close.

"What's not to like?" she murmured.

They kissed deeply until he let Quinn go so she could put on her hiking boots, then he helped her with her jacket and took her hand as they walked to his car.

After Caden settled behind the steering wheel, he turned to Quinn. "I'm sorry I moved so fast last night. It wasn't my intention." He paused. "I don't mean this as an excuse, but it's been a while since I was with a woman, and I've been attracted to you since that day in Cambridge. Forgive me?"

"Of course! Even though we talked about it afterward, I still spent half the night worried you thought I was some kind of nerd for slowing things down. Clearly, the desire was there for both of us."

He leaned in to kiss her. "You're the furthest thing from a nerd I've ever seen. And I swore off casual sex over a year ago." He reached over and smoothed her hair. "No matter how deep the connection, there is something about doing it on the first date that screams *casual* to me. I lost track of that last night."

Quinn nodded. "So, we're good?"

"I think we're great."

Quinn

Dry leaves littered the path in front of them, and bits of ice clung to the ledge bracketing the trail, the early harbingers of winter. A mournful train whistle sounded in the distance, a reminder they were still close to civilization. The air was crisp and cold, and Quinn pulled on a beanie to keep her ears warm.

She exhaled, her breath a white fog in front of her. She looked Caden up and down, realizing for the first time what he had on. "You're wearing sneakers? And a baseball cap? You're going to freeze."

He held up his hands. "I did not plan to go hiking. I brought swim trunks and my skates, but no hiking boots. And what's wrong with my cap? Please don't tell me you're a Yankees fan. We'll be over before we start!" He eyed her in mock dismay.

She shrugged. "Actually, I love the Red Sox."

His eyes twinkled. "Great! I'll be fine." They walked west toward Vermont. Because it was late in the year, they had the trail mostly to themselves, encountering only a handful of other hikers.

They walked in silence for a few minutes before Caden said, "This is nice. It's pretty and so quiet."

Quinn nodded. "But you need to see it in the summer or during the fall when the leaves are changing color. Now, *that's* when it's pretty."

Caden put his arm over Quinn's shoulder. "I hope I get a chance to do that."

She pulled him to a stop, grinning. Going up on tiptoe, she kissed him.

When they resumed walking, Caden asked what it was like growing up in rural Vermont.

Quinn snickered. "Just think of a Hallmark movie."

"I've never watched the Hallmark Channel."

She snickered again. "You don't know what you're missing. Essentially, I grew up in a small town where everyone knows your business. You couldn't get a cold without all your neighbors knowing. Even worse, my mother taught fifth grade, and my dad was the middle school principal in the town next to ours. I was a good kid, never got into any trouble, and I think part of the reason for that was because I knew my parents would find out in minutes if I pulled any shenanigans."

"How small?"

"Around five thousand people. My high school class had a hundred students."

Caden whistled. "Wow. Is that why you went so far away to college?"

"It was a big factor. I wanted to spread my wings, be somewhere no one knew me. I was shy and awkward in high school, so I wanted to reinvent myself."

"And did you?"

"Not totally." Her shoulders tensed, as they often did when she thought of that time. "I was still shy, just a little less awkward. College is more accepting of your quirks than high school. What about you? What was it like growing up in Boston?"

"Well, my high school class had three times as many kids as yours. I learned early on how to get around the city on the subway—the T, as we natives call it. Church every Sunday until I was old enough to say no. Or if there was a travel-hockey tournament. Hockey trumped church every time." He laughed, and Quinn joined him.

"I know about the T," she said. "My parents and I used to travel to Boston a few times a year when I was growing up. Take in a Red Sox game, visit the museums, walk around Boston

Common and Quincy Market. Maybe our paths crossed on one of those visits."

Caden smiled. "I like that idea."

"Me too. Where did you go to college?"

"Boston University. I received a significant scholarship and busted my ass to get into med school."

"Did you live at home?"

Caden snorted. "God no. I didn't want to leave the city, but I definitely wanted to leave home. I lived in a dorm and then an apartment with my best friends."

Quinn smiled. "I bet you were one of the popular kids, you handsome hockey player. Did you play anything else?" She kicked a rock in their path, sending it tumbling in front of them.

Caden mimicked her, sending the stone farther down the trail. "Yeah, soccer and baseball. You told me you ski and swim. Did you do them competitively in high school or college?"

"Just high school. I was on the varsity teams. Skiing was my favorite. What was yours?"

"Hockey, by far."

After they had been on the trail for about an hour, they came across a large rock outcropping with a path winding around it. Quinn scrambled to the top, and Caden snapped a picture of her.

"You need to come up here," she called down. "There's a bit of a view."

As he started toward her, a hiker passed by, and Caden asked if she'd wait and take a picture of them. She agreed, and he handed her his phone. After she snapped the picture, she left his phone on a rock at the side of the trail.

Quinn wrapped her arms around Caden, wanting to kiss him while they were on top of the boulder. Caden backed them away from the edge before bringing his lips to Quinn's.

"Your kisses go all the way to my toes every time," Quinn murmured. "I like that."

"I'm feeling the same thing."

They climbed down and looked at the picture.

"It's good," Quinn said, pleased. You never know what you are going to get when you asked a stranger to take a picture. "Will you text it to me?"

They walked another fifteen minutes, then turned around. They kissed again before starting back. Quinn's lips were chilled against Caden's, and he gathered her close.

Quinn settled against him and put her hands on his ears, which were like ice. "Caden. I'd be in agony if I didn't have a beanie on."

"I'm fine. All those years in ice arenas made me indifferent to the cold. But I have a confession." He made a face. "I'm not the biggest fan of high places."

"So you weren't wild about being up there, and that's why you backed away from the edge before you kissed me. I'm sorry. Does that mean you won't go mountain-climbing with me?"

Caden shrugged. "I'll climb mountains with you, but don't expect me to get near the edge of a cliff. Anything you're afraid of?"

Quinn hesitated, but he'd been open with her. It was only right to do the same. "I'm very claustrophobic. Like if we come across a cave, I won't be able to go into it. Merely the thought of being confined takes my breath away."

"Okay, you win the phobia contest. The thought of being up high doesn't bother me, just actually being there. I'll remember, no caves." Caden smiled at her reassuringly. "On a totally different subject, here's a funny story for you. Remember how I told you I asked Claire to run interference with my mother?"

Quinn nodded.

"Well, she made up a college classmate whom I had dinner with last night. I don't think my mother bought it, and it's probably driving her nuts."

Quinn frowned. "Are you hiding me?"

"Not hiding, but I want to keep you to myself for a little while." He took her hands in his. "I told you how my mom has no boundaries. She'd want to meet you and know everything about you. She'd be all over me. Do you mind?"

"No, I like the idea of being in a bubble that's just you and me. I've only mentioned you to one of my friends." She laughed. "Although your visit to the hospital on Friday kind of let the cat out of the bag."

"I told my best friend about you the day after we met. He and one other friend know we've been talking. I didn't tell them I was seeing you this weekend, but they'll figure it out." He leaned in to kiss her. "I can't get enough of you."

Quinn melted against him. "I feel the same way." When Caden let go of her, she asked, "What about your unmarried sisters? Is your mom all up in their business too? Do they have boyfriends?"

"Chloe does. They've been together for a few years, and it won't be a surprise if they get engaged soon. And yes, my mom is an equal-opportunity hoverer."

Quinn thought of something and tilted her head. "But wait, you told your best friend about me the day after we met, then didn't contact me until two weeks later? What's up with that?"

He winced. "Actually, I called you twice the next evening, but I didn't leave a message. I hoped you'd recognize my number and maybe call back." He looked sheepish. "That night I finally texted you? One of my friends told me my messages to him had been showing up as private. I felt like an idiot."

Quinn laughed. "I remember that!"

"True confession? You scared me. I felt a connection, and I wasn't sure I was ready for where it might lead." His voice was soft. "I spent those two weeks totally overthinking whether I should reach out to you."

She took his hands. "That connection hit me, too. I thought you were blowing smoke about taking me to dinner. I'm glad you weren't." Standing on her tiptoes, she kissed him.

Chapter Twelve

Irish Coffee and Foot Rubs

Quinn

THE DRIVE BACK TO the town house wasn't long enough for them to warm up. Quinn said she was going to make them something to drink, but ran upstairs to her bedroom first. She came back and threw a pair of thick socks at Caden.

"Catch! I ended up with two pairs of these." She showed him she was wearing an identical pair. "I think they've been waiting in my closet for you to be here with cold feet."

Caden grinned and began putting them on. Quinn beamed at him before heading to the kitchen. After a moment, she heard him light the fire, then come to the kitchen. He leaned on the counter, watching her make the same drinks as the night before.

She handed him one, and they walked to the living room. Caden motioned toward the end of the couch, telling her to sit there as he sat toward the other end, and pulled her legs onto his lap. She shivered a little.

"Are your feet ticklish?" he asked.

I like where this is going. "No."

Caden removed one sock and gently started massaging her foot. Quinn instantly felt the sensation in her lady parts and struggled to stay still.

"Do you like that?"

She sighed. "Oh yes."

He continued to massage, thumbs rubbing more deeply and turning her on even more. The struggle to stay quiet became more difficult as desire washed over her.

He grinned. "You sure you're not ticklish?"

"Nope, not ticklish."

She watched the realization hit Caden. "Oh, this is an erogenous zone for you."

A moan escaped Quinn's lips. "Yes! Totally!"

Caden's eyes lit with a devilish twinkle, and the foot rub continued as he lavished care on each toe. Quinn knew he was thoroughly enjoying watching her.

Moving to the other foot, he asked, "Both feet have the same reaction?"

"Yes." She covered her face with her hands. "I'm embarrassed."

"Don't be. Watching you is sexy." He shifted his hips and sighed. "And you're right, these socks are amazing. My feet have totally thawed out."

After he had massaged every inch of her feet, he put her socks back on, swung her legs to the floor, and moved over next to her. She smiled and slid her arms around his back, parting her lips, inviting his tongue into her mouth. They continued to play with each other until the timer on Quinn's stove sounded.

Caden groaned as he let her go.

They went into the kitchen, where Quinn gave him plates and silverware and directed him to the table while she prepared the rest of their dinner, spaghetti with garlic bread and a salad. After setting the table, he picked up the bottle of red wine on the counter. "Want me to open this?"

"Please."

When they were settled at the table, Caden took a mouthful of the spaghetti. "My God, this is delicious!"

"It's my specialty. I'm glad you like it."

As they ate, they talked. She asked him where he'd done his residency.

"Mass General." He grabbed another piece of garlic bread.

"So you've always lived in Boston?"

"Yes, although technically I lived out in Natick, west of the city, for a while. Remember, I told you I had a lengthy commute before I bought the brownstone?"

Quinn nodded. "That's so foreign to me. I couldn't wait to leave my hometown."

He shrugged. "I like Boston. It has everything I want. Maybe it's the difference between growing up in a small town and growing up in a city. Of the places you've lived, which did you like the best?"

"I liked them all, but honestly, I've only felt like I was home since I've been at Dartmouth. The South wasn't me, and neither was the Northwest. I guess I'm a New Englander at heart."

"That's how I feel too." He smiled. "I just didn't have to leave to figure it out."

She smiled back. "I love Boston. Maybe I wouldn't have wanted to leave if I'd grown up there."

Quinn finished her wine and started to get up, but Caden reached over, gently pushing her back into her chair. "My mom's rules. The person who cooks doesn't have to clean up. So sit down, and I'll take care of things. I might need some direction about where things go."

Quinn watched in fascination as Caden made his way around her kitchen. He opened and closed cabinet doors as he cleaned, grinning at her as it took him three tries to find the correct place for an unused bowl.

Afterward, he refilled both their wine glasses and extended his hand to pull her out of her chair. They searched her streaming services for a movie and finally settled on a scary one Quinn had seen before. She didn't want to watch a new movie because she had a suspicion they wouldn't end up seeing much of it.

And she was right. Not five minutes into the movie, their mouths found each other. His hands cradled the back of her head, bringing her closer to him. They explored each other's mouths, and eventually he lowered her down to the couch just like the night before, but this time, his hands stayed on the outside of her clothes. She loved the weight of him against her.

By the time the movie ended, between kissing, conversation, and refilling wine glasses, they had seen basically none of it.

A perfect movie night, in Quinn's opinion.

"I'm leaving early in the morning. Probably around nine. My dad wants to be back before noon." Caden stoked her hair.

"So I won't see you tomorrow."

"No." He sighed. "How's next weekend look? I know you said you have plans."

"I have a cookie swap with my friends on Sunday, so Saturday I need to bake." Quinn caressed his cheek before leaning in to kiss him.

"Do you need a sous-chef?"

Quinn smirked. "I don't know. What are your qualifications?"

"I'm good at weights and measures, take direction well and wield a mean spoon. I could stitch up a broken gingerbread man too."

Quinn giggled. "Okay, you're hired. I won't even check your references. Will you come up Friday night?" She stroked his leg.

"Probably, although I think my dad's going to ride with me, so I don't know how early I'll be able to leave. I'll work it out this week and let you know."

With the logistics out of the way, they went back to making out. They got lost in each other all over again, and in no time, it was after midnight. They reluctantly parted and walked to the door.

She put her arms around him. "This has been a great weekend. One of the best I've had in a long time."

"For me too."

They kissed deeply, then she stood in the open door, watching him walk to his car, missing him already.

Quinn shut the door and leaned against it, thinking about his lips on hers and the weight of his body against her. Admitting to him how much the weekend had meant to her was an enormous step forward for her. He made her feel safe and cared for, although a small part of her was still afraid he was too good to be real. She made her way to bed, knowing her dreams would be happy ones.

Just after she lay down, Quinn's phone rang.

"I enjoyed last night and today." Caden's voice caressed her.

"Me too. I wasn't exaggerating when I said it was one of my best weekends."

"Neither was I. I'm sorry I have to leave early. I'll talk to you sometime tomorrow."

When she put her phone down, she was smiling.

Chapter Thirteen

The Robe

Caden

Caden woke up thinking about the sweetness of Quinn's lips, then he thought about her response when he talked about Claire having run interference for him. He didn't want Quinn to think he was hiding her. She'd seemed to understand once he explained things, but her words still bothered him.

That meant he needed to tell his mother about Quinn—and hope she wouldn't go overboard.

Everyone was enjoying scrambled eggs and sausage when he entered the main house.

His mother pounced on him immediately. "How was your evening?"

Joining them at the table, he grinned. "It was outstanding. How was the Chinese food?"

"Superb," James said. "There's a great new restaurant in town."

"Maybe I'll try it the next time I come up." Caden took a deep breath and looked at his mother. "So, Ma, about a month ago, I was at a conference, and I met a nurse who works at Dartmouth. We had dinner Friday night, and then we spent yesterday together." He took a breath. "I didn't tell you for a couple of reasons. First, I wasn't sure where it would go. And second, I want to get to know her with no outside pressure, no questions, no expectations."

His mother digested this. "And I would have done all that?"

"Yeah, you would have."

She looked around the table, and Claire nodded.

Caden took her hand. "Ma, we all love you, but you can be a little over the top with wanting every detail of our lives. We appreciate the love and support you give us, but sometimes we need to be left alone."

Rory cried softly from his cradle in the living room, and before Claire could get up, Mom left the table to tend to him. Dad frowned at Caden and followed her into the other room.

Claire looked at Caden. "Whoa, where'd all that come from?"

"It needed to be said." He paused. "Do you think she's pissed?"

Claire shrugged.

Mom and Dad returned with Rory and handed him to Claire to nurse. With a quiet word to Mom, Dad finished getting ready to leave.

Before they left, Caden squeezed Claire's shoulder. "I was hoping to hold him one more time, but I'll have to wait until next weekend." He shook James's hand and looked toward his mother before pulling her into a hug. "I really do love you."

She nodded, squeezing him. "I know. And I love you. No questions."

"Thank you."

Once on their way, Caden glanced over at his dad and said, "I need to make a stop before we get on the highway."

Caden: Are you up?

Quinn: Just barely. Are you on the road?

Caden: I'm in your parking lot. Can I come in for a minute?

Her answer took longer than he expected, but finally, a text came back.

Quinn: Yes, it's fine.

Caden looked up from his phone to see his dad watching him. Holding up a finger to indicate he wouldn't be long, he climbed out of the car and walked up to Quinn's door. She opened it, and he looked at her from top to bottom. Her hair was disheveled, and she was barefoot, wearing a short robe. He could see satin boxers peeking out below the robe.

"Damn. You are stunning." They embraced before he backed away to look at her again. "And incredibly sexy."

"I literally just woke up. I'm a wreck." Max pushed past her to rub against Caden's legs, meowing loudly for attention.

Caden kneeled down to pet him. "I'm glad to see you too, Max." Straightening, he stepped inside and shook his head. "Oh no, you are most definitely not a wreck." He unzipped his jacket and invited her to come closer. Folded in each other's arms, she buried her head in his chest. His heart was racing, and he could tell hers was doing the same. She stood on tiptoe to reach his lips. Their tongues twined, and they both moaned with desire.

"I wasn't expecting you," she murmured.

He eased his hold on her slightly. "I only wanted a hug and a kiss before I left town." He looked her up and down again. "That robe is really something. You've been all bundled up every other time I've seen you." He kissed her again. "Damn, I don't know what to say. I'm gobsmacked."

She laughed and put her arms around him again.

He savored the feel of her body against his. "I can't stay. My dad's in the car, and I told him I'd only be a few minutes. I told my mom—actually, I told all of them—that we went to dinner and spent yesterday together."

She cocked her head. "What happened to keeping me to yourself?"

"I didn't want you thinking I'm hiding you, because I am definitely not." He kissed her again, thrusting his tongue deep into her mouth.

She groaned and pressed herself more closely to him.

They reluctantly parted, and Quinn sighed, smiling. "Seeing you this morning is like the cherry on top of a sundae."

He ogled her, shook his head to clear his thoughts, and finally left, telling her he'd talk to her later.

As Caden steered toward the highway, his dad said, "You look hot and bothered."

Caden gave him a sideways glance and shook his head.

"I know you told your mother no questions, and I'm not asking questions. I'm making an observation," Dad said mildly. "I *observe* you looking hot and bothered. And happy. You look happy."

Caden drove a mile before answering. "I am happy... as well as hot and bothered."

They both laughed.

After another mile, Caden admitted, "I'm also scared." He didn't have to elaborate—his dad knew him well.

Dad shrugged. "It looks to me like the happy might be stronger than the scared. What happened with Mary was terrible, but it's been three years. It's time to move on."

"I've tried moving on, Dad."

"You went out with a bunch of women, but you haven't let yourself get close to anyone. And you hadn't even had a date in over a year!" His father waved his hand, dismissing Caden's words. "Until this weekend."

"How did you get so knowledgeable about my dating life?"

"You talk to Claire. Claire talks to your mother, and your mother talks to me. You know there are no secrets in this family. We worry about you."

Caden shook his head. "You don't need to worry about me. I'm fine."

"But scared." Dad smiled gently. "Don't let the fear paralyze you. It's obvious you care about whoever was on the other side of that door."

"Quinn. Her name's Quinn." He paused. "And yes, I care about her. We're seeing where it goes."

Caden called Claire when he got home. "You tell Ma what I've told you in confidence about dates I've had?" There was laughter in his voice.

"You know I'm powerless against her questions."

They both chuckled. Mom was a force to be reckoned with. "I hear you made a stop before you headed home."

"Geesh, I can't do anything in private!"

"Well, you had Dad with you. Did the weekend go well?"

"It went very well. She's... easy to be with. And I'm coming back up on Friday. Dad will ride up with me so he can convince Mom to go home with him. Everything going okay with you? Was she pissed about what I said?"

"All good, and it's a big help to have Mom here. But a week will be long enough. Plus, James will be on break after this week. And nothing has been said about your little announcement. I think Dad got to her."

"I hope so. Chloe and Chrissy are coming up to see you tomorrow. They want to meet their nephew."

"That's good. He wants to meet them." Claire laughed, and Caden joined her.

"Take care. I love you."

"Same."

Quinn

Ashley was waiting and had ordered two margaritas and nachos when Quinn slid into a chair at the Sidecar late on Sunday afternoon.

Quinn took a long sip of her drink before asking, "What's up? And thanks for this." She raised her glass.

"The ward was crazy with several new admissions, and one of the long-term patients took a turn for the worse. I hate how short-staffed we are on the weekends." Ashley sighed.

"I get the frustration. Wish I had some ideas about how to fix it."

"So, how was your weekend?" Ashley smiled. "You lucky thing, to have both days off."

Ashley wasn't working on Friday, so she hadn't seen Caden, but Quinn was sure she had heard about his impromptu visit from the other nurses.

"Well, I worked eight days straight, including Thanksgiving, and I'll be working Christmas Eve and Christmas Day. I've earned some weekends off." She sipped her drink, wondering how long it would take Ashley to get around to Quinn's mystery man.

Not long. "I heard you had a handsome visitor on Friday."

There it is. "For once, the rumor mill was correct. I did." Quinn giggled.

Ashley pounced. "Aha, you're blushing again! More wild and wonderful sex?"

"Actually, no." She laughed. "But it was a fantastic weekend. We went to dinner Friday night and hiked on Saturday. He's easy to be with." Quinn couldn't suppress a sly smile. *Very easy.*

"But no sex?"

"The attraction is there, but we both agree we aren't looking for casual." Thinking about Caden's body against hers, as always, made her tingle. Her phone rang, and Ashley nodded, indicating she should answer it. "Hello?"

"Hi, beautiful. Are you still wearing that robe?"

"I'm at a pub with my friend Ashley, so it wouldn't be appropriate." She grinned at Ashley, whose eyes were wide.

"You're right. It's only appropriate if I'm there to see it." She laughed.

Caden laughed too. "I know I sound like a Neanderthal. Enjoy your evening and call me when you get home. Please."

Quinn changed into the robe and snapped some selfies before calling Caden.

He answered on the first ring. "Seeing your name on the display gets me going."

"I know what you mean. Calling you started my heart racing. How was your drive home?"

"My dad thought I looked hot and bothered."

"Were you? Hot and bothered?"

"Oh yeah. And if it subsided, all I had to do was picture you in that robe and it started all over again."

"I wish you were here, holding me."

"I'm wishing the same thing."

Chapter Fourteen

Lying Under the Christmas Tree

Quinn

ON MONDAY MORNING, QUINN awoke to a good-morning text from Caden and responded by sending a picture in the robe.

For the rest of the week, there continued to be a text waiting for her every morning, and they spoke every night at ten thirty.

On Tuesday night, Quinn cried, telling him about the death of one of her favorite patients. He responded with empathy, telling her he wished he was there to wipe the tears away.

On Wednesday, she told him she was going to pick up a Christmas tree the next day. He asked her to wait until Friday night, and she agreed, touched that he wanted to join her.

On Thursday, there was a package in her mail with a Boston return address. She tore it open and found a print of the picture from their hike on Saturday. It was in a frame that exactly matched her other hiking pictures and bore a sticky note on it that said, *Quinn, I want a place in your gallery. Caden.* There was a heart following his name.

She immediately found a hammer and nail to hang it up.

When they spoke that night, she let him know how the gift had touched her. "It was a great surprise, and I love it. Thank you!"

"I'm glad you like it." She could hear his smile in the words.

Friday finally arrived, and after work, Quinn showered and dressed in jeans and a heavy sweater. She paced, waiting for Caden, hoping their time together would be as magical as it had been the week before.

As soon as she opened the door for him, he swept her into his arms, and relief mixed with a healthy dose of desire washed over her. Their long, lingering kiss lasted until his stomach growled.

Quinn laughed. "I'm hungry too. Let's get burgers before we go to the Christmas tree lot."

She grabbed her keys, and he asked what she was doing.

"We're not putting a tree in your gorgeous car. We're taking my car. They made Subarus for this."

He argued, but Quinn smirked. "Just give up. You will not win."

As they ate their burgers, they talked logistics. He asked if they were going to cut the tree themselves.

"No, I'm happy to let someone else do the cutting."

They finished eating and drove to the tree lot. She selected a tree quickly, and they bundled it into her car.

Caden carried it into the town house, where the stand, lights, and decorations were already out. He put it in the stand and started draping the lights, pausing after a minute to ask if she minded him doing it.

"Not at all." She grinned. "Two years ago was the first time I had my own tree, and I watched YouTube videos to figure out the lights. But you are doing fine."

As she watched him work, she got curious. He had told her earlier he didn't put up a tree for himself, but clearly, he'd done plenty of tree decorating at some point.

She draped the beads, and they hung the decorations together, chatting along the way. As Caden hung the final ornament, Quinn turned off all the lights so they could admire their work. He reminisced about lying under the tree as a child to look up at the lights.

"I did the same thing!" Quinn exclaimed.

He picked up the blanket from the couch and spread it under the tree. "Let's try it."

They laughed as they arranged themselves under the tree. "This was easier when we were smaller," Quinn mock groused.

Once they were comfortable, they lay on their backs, enjoying the glow of the lights. Caden turned to her, and supporting himself over her, kissed her gently. She put her hands on his neck to bring him closer.

"Does this bother you?" he murmured.

"You mean because of claustrophobia?"

He nodded.

"It depends on the circumstance. I'm okay with being on the bottom," she said with a grin.

"I wasn't sure. It's tight down here with the tree over us. But very romantic."

She rolled them so they were both on their sides with their arms around each other. It wasn't bad, but... "We might be more comfortable on the couch," she finally whispered.

"Oh, you have no romantic soul." He extricated himself from under the tree and reached for her hands, tugging her to her feet. They sat on the couch and kissed deeply.

Eventually, she drew back, cupping her hands around both sides of his face. "Thank you for remembering about the claustrophobia and asking if I was okay. No one's ever done that."

"Does it bother you to be held down? I picture it as an issue."

"Yes, exactly! Lying together isn't a problem, but being pinned down freaks me out." She looked away before continuing, debating if she wanted to expose so much of herself. She decided she could trust Caden. "I was with a guy who, after he found out I didn't like it, would put me in that situation."

"And you stayed with him?"

"For a while."

Caden put his arms around her, holding her tightly. "It makes me angry that someone would do that to you. And sad that you would put up with it."

"Yeah, I was stupid. I stayed a couple of months longer than I should have, and that's why when I started here, I stopped looking for a relationship. When it comes to guys, my choices have been... poor."

"I'd like to think you were waiting for me." His voice was soft and warm, wrapping her in affection.

She leaned into him. "I'd like to think that, too."

"I know there are women who get off on being mistreated. It kills me to ask, but is that you? Because I can't do that."

"Oh, God no, not at all!" Quinn shook her head vigorously. "It was a turnoff. But I felt somehow it was all I deserved. I put up with scraps from him so I wouldn't be alone." Tears filled her eyes. "I went to therapy," she said after a moment. "I still go to therapy, and I don't think I'd let myself stay in a situation like that again."

He stroked her hair, then quietly said, "I see a therapist."

Quinn tried not to let Caden see her surprise. He seemed so together—but that was always the way for people like them. "I believe everyone can benefit from therapy. We all have something. But you know what I've learned in the last few weeks? Being treated well is a real turn-on." At his intense gaze, she grinned. "I feel like my body's on fire all the time, even when I'm not with you. And with you here..." She stroked his cheek.

He leaned his head over and kissed her, stroking his hands up and down her back and finding his way under her sweater.

She sighed and worked her hands under his shirt as well. His hand came around to the front and brushed her breast. She jumped, and he paused.

"Okay?"

"Yes." She was sure he wouldn't go further than she was comfortable with.

His hands were warm on her skin, gently caressing her. "What's the temperature of that fire now?" His low, sexy voice made her shiver.

"It's a three-alarm, for sure." She moved against him. "I'd say five-alarm, but I know there's more you can do to me to take it up even further."

He grinned. "What you said before about being on fire all day? I'm feeling the same thing. And I'm thoroughly enjoying it, although having an erection at work can be awkward some-times."

She shook her head, laughing. "Oh, you poor man. Your arousal is out there for everyone to see. I have it easier, although I blush at random times throughout the day, which attracts attention."

After another extended kiss, he said he should go. "What time should I be here for baking?"

"One o'clock," Quinn said, embracing him tightly at her door.

She watched until his car was out of sight. Walking to her bedroom, she still tingled from his touch. *Why did I think about my time in Seattle? I thought I had shed all the tears I had about that.*

After climbing into bed, she pulled her vibrator out of the nightstand drawer. The desire Caden stirred would not subside by itself. It took no time at all for her to find an orgasm, imagining the whole time how it would feel with Caden inside her.

Caden

Caden's erection from his make-out session with Quinn still throbbed as he walked into the guesthouse. He slid his jeans off, relieved to let his cock spring free. Even though it was after midnight, he started a cold shower, which did nothing to relieve him.

Switching to hot water, he took his erection in hand, stroking himself to an orgasm in only a couple of minutes. *God, I hope I last longer than this when Quinn and I finally make love.*

Make love?

Smiling, he toweled dry.

When he called Quinn, her voice was low and sexy as she purred, "Hi."

Trying to match her, he murmured, "You have gotten under my skin."

"Tell me more."

"I was still hot and bothered after the drive here."

"What'd you do about it?" Her voice was becoming lighter, but it still turned him on.

"Took a cold shower."

"Brrrrr. Did it help?"

"No."

"Did you jerk off?"

Caden loved having her talk to him like this. He tried to come up with a smart reply, but before he could, Quinn continued.

"You know, they say that will make you go blind," she teased.

"I've heard that."

"If it does, we'll be blind together."

Fuck me now. His cock jumped to attention at her words. "You too?" he spit out.

"Yup."

"Fingers or vibrator?" He had to know.

"Vibe. I needed something inside me."

Caden groaned. "You're killing me. And... I'm all hot and bothered again."

"Me too." She chuckled. "Sleep tight."

"You too. Hey, Quinn, you better warn Max he's going to have to share your bed with me soon."

145

Chapter Fifteen

The Christmas Village

Caden

CADEN ARRIVED ON TIME the next day to find Quinn's kitchen littered with baking paraphernalia. Cookie sheets, parchment paper, flour, sugar, and spices covered the counters. He asked what they were making, and Quinn told him sugar cookies using her grandmother's recipe, plus nutmeg logs and rum balls.

"Rum balls? Now, those sound interesting."

"Yeah, they're popular, and I'm the only one who brings what we consider an adult treat. We'll make the sugar cookies first so they can cool and be ready for frosting after we finish the others."

Caden did what she asked as they worked together and proved that his stirring skills were epic. They made a good team. Along the way, he asked about the cookie swap.

"It was already a thing when I started at Dartmouth, and they invited me. It's a large group, probably fifteen or more adults plus kids. There are new people every year."

"Morning or afternoon?"

"It's in the morning because the kids are best then. I think they tried it in the afternoon, but it ran up against nap time. It's kinda chaotic."

"So you'll be spent afterwards?"

"You're remembering what I told you after Friendsgiving?"

"Yeah. You said big social things exhaust you."

She smiled. "I'm going to have to watch what I say to you if you are going to remember everything. And yes, I'll have a good time, but I'll be happy to get back to my quiet home."

"I don't have to leave early tomorrow. Can I stop by?"

"I'd like that." After they finished, she poured them each a shot of rum, and they walked to the couch. He enjoyed his shot, then, remembering how well the foot rub had gone before, swung her legs onto his lap and began massaging her feet.

She squirmed. "Oh, you know what that does to me."

He grinned. "Figure your feet must be tired. Relax and en-joy." He took out his phone, scrolled to pictures of a light dis-play he'd found, handed it to her, and went back to rubbing her feet. "I found this light display in Woodstock, Vermont and thought it might be fun to take a drive over. It's not too far is it?"

Earlier in the week, when he'd searched for seasonal decorations, he'd wondered how he would react. *Can I do that? Walk through a park filled with Christmas lights?* Quinn was into the holidays, and he knew his avoidance of all things Christmas might be a problem. *It's time for this to stop.*

"About half an hour and I'd love that." She handed him back his phone. "I've seen pictures before and thought about going but haven't."

"We should leave soon. I found a restaurant to try too."

"Okay, but can we do this for a few more minutes, please?" Quinn begged.

Caden laughed and nodded, pulling her over to his lap to kiss her before getting back to her feet.

Quinn chatted as they made the drive, remarking about every light display they saw along the way. Caden responded to her but didn't initiate conversation, knowing he was more subdued than usual, but hoping she wouldn't notice. Instead, he concentrated on his breathing, attempting to keep his emotions under control.

He parked the car and put his arm around her as they walked toward the entrance. Her closeness brought him comfort. As they turned the corner to enter, a riot of color assaulted their eyes. Caden drew in a sharp breath as Quinn exclaimed, "Oh my God, this is amazing!" The evergreen trees were strung with multicolored lights while the bare branches of every hardwood tree were wrapped in white mini lights, and lighted candy canes outlined the paths.

She looked at him with delight. "I love this. It's like walking through a fairyland!"

Caden had already taken several deep breaths, and he told himself to latch on to Quinn's enthusiasm. "It's beautiful. Let's see what more there is."

As they walked, Quinn had her phone out to take pictures. They passed a grove of evergreens, each one lit in a different color, then they encountered inflatables of all the characters in *Rudolph the Red-Nosed Reindeer.*

Quinn snapped more pictures. "Growing up, this was my favorite Christmas special."

"Which character was your favorite?"

"I always like Yukon Cornelius."

Caden nudged her toward the figure. "Let me take your picture with him."

Quinn mugged for the camera and Caden relaxed more as he watched her.

"Look, there's more." Caden motioned ahead. It was getting easier. "It's like an inflatable village. I always liked the Peanuts special."

"That's in second place for me. Did you have a favorite character?"

"Linus, because I like his speech."

Together they said, "That's what Christmas is all about, Charlie Brown." Caden laughed, and gathered Quinn into a hug.

The Peanuts characters were all gathered around Snoopy's doghouse and Quinn made Caden pose for a picture. Then she asked, "Want to take one with the Grinch?"

"Why, do I seem grinchy?" *I'm enjoying this. Surely she can see that.*

"Not at all. But the Grinch is the only one near your height."

"I'll pass."

Caden spied mistletoe as they passed under an arch. He kissed her before pointing over their heads. "Can't miss a chance to kiss you."

They were nearing the end when they ran into a long line of families with small children. Caden looked ahead. "There's a gingerbread village coming up. I think we can keep going." He took her hand, and as they walked past the line, he could see the kids were waiting to have a picture taken with Santa. He paused. "Do you want to sit on Santa's lap?"

She grinned and stood on tiptoe to whisper in his ear. "I'd rather sit on yours."

He slid his arm over her shoulder, pulling her close to him again. "Don't tease me like that."

They shared a smile, and she mouthed, "Later."

As he opened the car door for her, she threw her arms around him. "That was so much fun! Thank you for thinking about it. I loved it!"

After dropping Quinn at her town house, he thought about her enthusiasm with a smile. He'd had fun too.

Maybe tonight will rewire my brain as far as Christmas lights go. He fell asleep, hoping visions of sugarplums would dance in his dreams.

He wandered through the house, looking for Mary, happy to be home early to spend time with her before they went out. Approaching the bedroom, he thought he heard a man moaning. He opened the door, and there she was, naked, with a strange man under her.

Caden fought his way back to consciousness, his heart pounding. *It's a dream, a dream, a dream! Open your eyes—open them!*

Breathless, he sat up, heart still racing. *So much for rewiring my brain. Fuck! How long is this going to keep happening?*

He slumped back down onto his pillow, and gradually sleep overtook him.

But in the morning, his first thought was about the nightmare. *Am I being fair to Quinn, pursuing a relationship with her? What the fuck is going to happen if we sleep together and I wake up screaming like a banshee?*

He didn't have the dream every night, though. And he'd slept with plenty of women during his online-dating phase without incident.

I'm going with that. I will not stop seeing her. My feelings are too strong to give her up.

That afternoon, Caden rang Quinn's doorbell, carrying a present that he hoped she'd like. Once he stepped inside, he set the small bag on the bench in the entryway so his arms could envelop her fully. She melted into them.

"Let's go sit down," Quinn whispered in his ear. "I've been standing all morning."

Caden grabbed the bag before they made their way to the living room. They were all over each other before they even sat down.

"I loved last night," she murmured, "but there wasn't enough of this."

"I know. But I knew if we were here all night, I'd completely lose my resolve." He paused. "I went to a Christmas fair this morning with Claire and James. I bought you something." He removed a fairy ornament from the bag. "It's as close as I could find to a druid."

"I love it!" She grinned. "Thank you. I love how you remember everything I say. I have something for you, too." She ran to the kitchen and came back with a coffee cup ornament. It was personalized, etched with *November 5th*.

"The day I bought you the chai." His whole body lit up with warmth. "Thank you. Can we hang them on your tree?"

They hung them, and Caden asked if she wanted to lie under the tree and look at the lights again.

She laughed. "No, let's stick to the couch."

Caden picked up where he left off on Friday night: his hands under her sweater, stroking her breast, while his tongue explored her mouth.

Her hand wandered down his stomach until it touched his erection. *Oh damn.* This was more than Quinn had done before, and he hoped she would keep going. Her fingers stroking him on top of his jeans brought groans of pleasure from him.

Sliding his hand down the outside of her jeans, he reached between her legs, rubbing lightly. Her hips moved against him as she gasped.

He proceeded slowly, confident Quinn would stop him if he made her uncomfortable. He unzipped her jeans and snaked his hand inside and moaned when she did the same to him and he felt her hand on his cock through his boxers. *Oh yes.*

Caden could feel her heat, and he wished her hand would move to the inside of his boxers. Gaining control of himself, he groaned and withdrew his hand. "You seriously turn me on so much."

She zipped his jeans and leaned against him. "I know. I feel I've lost all rational thought. Do you think we've moved beyond casual?"

"I really like you, Quinn. I like this, but I also enjoyed cooking with you and looking at Christmas lights with you." He smiled. "That's part of the reason I wanted to do that last night, to see if there's more than the physical attraction."

She nodded. "There is for me. I love being with you, getting your texts or talking on the phone. I'm more comfortable with you than I've ever been with a guy."

That made his heart leap. "Are you saying you're ready to take this further?" He punctuated his question with a kiss.

"I think so?" Caden could hear the question in her voice, but she added, "I'm saying I like you. I like you a lot. And damn, you reach deep into me."

"I feel the same way," he said, leaning his head against hers. "And I'm definitely feeling like we've moved beyond casual. How's next weekend looking?" Caden hoped she was going to be available.

"I'm going to dinner with my friends on Friday night, then the weekend is open. Will you come up again?"

"Yes, I'll be up on Friday night." He was ready to spend the night with her, and he hoped she was ready, too. "You could come over to the guesthouse after your dinner... and stay. If that's okay with Max."

She smiled. "I'd like that. And Max will be okay overnight."

He zipped her jeans, then slid her onto his lap, burying his face in her neck and nibbling on her ear. She shifted her hips to get comfortable, bringing him to attention again. They continued playing with each other, pushing boundaries and pulling back, until Caden realized the time.

Chapter Sixteen

Sam Needs A Friend

Quinn

ON MONDAY NIGHT, QUINN relaxed with a glass of wine and a playlist, thinking about her time with Caden. And about her growing feelings.

I'm falling in love with him.

She had felt it since his impromptu stop the Sunday before, and this weekend only intensified everything. *How on earth did I go from not allowing any men in my life less than two months ago to falling in love?*

Quinn knew the time with Sam had opened the door for her. Hearing the truth about their breakup when she was nineteen had finally banished the self-doubts she'd dealt with for years. And the physical contact they'd shared had awoken the desire she'd kept tamped down since she left Seattle. Sam wasn't her future, but she was grateful for what her brief time with him had given her. *Maybe some day I'll get to tell him that.*

Does Caden feel the same? I'm not sure, but I'm all in. If it ends, I'll have to deal with that, but for now, I'm going to enjoy every minute.

Quinn's phone startled her when it rang as she was eating dinner on Tuesday. Caden never called before ten thirty. Her heart stopped when she saw who it was. *Oh God.*

She answered and asked tentatively, "Sam?"

"Hey, Quinn." His voice was slurred. "I could use a friend to talk to."

"Have you been drinking?"

"Why, yes. Yes, I have been, or rather, I am. I think I'm near you—that's why I called. And because you're my friend—you are my friend, right?"

She sighed. "Where are you?"

"I'm at the Sidecar."

Just across the river in Vermont. Damn it. "I can be there in about fifteen minutes. Don't go anywhere." She ended the call and jammed her feet into her shoes while Max watched. As she threw on a sweater, she looked at the cat and shook her head. "I told you he was needy. I only hope he doesn't drive somewhere."

Luckily, the bar wasn't very busy, so Sam was easy to locate. She slid into a chair next to him. "After we drank so much in Boston that night, didn't you swear off drinking like that ever again? Looks like you didn't even last a month."

"I didn't last long at all after you bowed out of my life." He smirked. "You could say I am not adjusting well to being alone. I have consumed copious amounts of alcohol."

"So what's going on tonight that made you call me? I thought I made it clear we shouldn't stay in touch, at least for a while. And why are you in White River?"

"Norah and I went to mediation today. Did you know that at the end of a relationship, you get to go to mediation? It's great fun." He signaled the server to bring him another beer. "The mediator's office is near here. At the end, the only thing I wanted was a drink. Actually, several drinks. And then I thought about you." He took a long swallow of his beer. "So, I called."

While she tried to figure out what to say, he gazed at her. Finally, he looked away. "I didn't think you'd come."

Sam didn't seem as drunk in person as he had sounded on the phone. She probably shouldn't have come. *Always the needy ones.* "You said you needed a friend to talk to, and you sounded drunk. I'm concerned for your safety."

He laughed sarcastically. "Concerned for my safety, how formal! I *am* drunk and need a friend to talk to." He told her about the mediation session, how they discussed a schedule for Piper to be with each of them, how they would split the holidays, how they would take care of selling the house, and other financial obligations.

His anger was palpable, and Quinn remarked on it.

"Hell yes, I'm angry," he snarled. "I don't want any of this. Piper shuttling back and forth between us, not getting to see her at Thanksgiving, selling the house I put so much time into. It all sucks." He finished his beer and raised his hand for another.

Quinn reached out to pull it down. "You should stop."

He stared at her and shrugged off her hand. She thought he might argue with her, but instead, he put his head down on the table.

When he looked up, his eyes were red. "I've been a prick to Norah. She drops Piper off, and I don't say a word to her." He swallowed. "She's being generous with me, paying her part of the mortgage, at least for a while, and inviting me to stay at her place on Christmas Eve so we'll both be there with Piper on Christmas morning. She looked so sad this afternoon. But the anger comes over me in waves." His fists clenched.

Quinn wasn't sure what to say. His house was twenty miles away on winding dirt roads—she doubted an Uber would take him. "You shouldn't drive home. You can stay in my guest room."

He protested, but Quinn was not giving in. After speaking to the owner of the bar, who said Sam's car would be fine until morning, she went back to the table where Sam was standing, unsteady but upright. He staggered as he followed her to her car, and Quinn knew she'd made the right decision.

Once they walked into the townhouse, Quinn led Sam to her kitchen and directed him to the table. "Sit down. I'm going to make you something to eat."

Quinn glanced at the clock, knowing Caden would call soon. She bit her lip and picked up her phone.

> Quinn: Hey, a friend is having a bit of a crisis tonight. I can't talk to you.

> Caden: Hope everything's okay. I'll talk to you tomorrow. You can call if you have a moment.

Sam ate the food she put in front of him and then pushed the plate away. He reached his hand across the table, placing it on Quinn's arm. "I miss you. Remember how good it was being together in Boston? I'm thinking about it all the time." He rubbed his hand on her skin. "Want to taste you again, want to make you moan, want to be inside you again. Do you think about it?"

Quinn pulled her arm away. "No." She hoped her crisp reply left no doubt. "I'm going to clean up, and then I'll show you the guest room. You need to sleep off the alcohol." They both rose from the table, and Sam wandered into the living room.

After a moment, Sam came back to the kitchen, carrying the picture of Quinn and Caden on the hike. "Is this the doctor we met in Boston?"

Her eyes widened. "What the hell are you doing? You had no business taking that off the wall!" She reached for it.

Sam took a step back. "How'd you get..." Before he could finish, he tripped and dropped the frame. It crashed to the floor, shattering the glass. He bent to pick it up. "Shit! I'm sorry, I didn't mean—"

"Shut up!" Quinn shoved him away. "I don't care what you meant!" She picked up the frame and held it close before placing it on the table.

Sam stood, silent, as Quinn swept up the glass. When she was satisfied there was nothing left on the floor to cut Max's paws, she looked up at Sam with fury in her eyes. "You're nothing but a drunk! I should take you back to the Sidecar and dump you." She took a deep, shaky breath. "But I don't want to be responsible if you have an accident and kill yourself. Or worse, someone else."

Quinn led him to the guest room. "Good night."

She was closing the door as Sam tried again to apologize. "I'm so sorry..."

"Go to sleep, Sam. I'm not interested in your hollow apologies."

She stomped back to her own room, still fuming.

I shouldn't have brought him here. Why do I continue to rescue people? Caden is the first man I've been involved with who has himself together, and I'm probably going to blow it.

Sam. She hadn't told him everything about Sam.

I must tell him Sam stayed here. I will not hide this from him. And I'll pick up new glass for the picture. She pulled on sweatpants and a long-sleeved T-shirt, but she was still shaking with anger as she crawled under the covers. *That picture is one of the most thoughtful things I've ever been given. That asshole! Thank God the frame and photo are okay.*

There was a text from Caden waiting in the morning.

> *Caden: Hope your friend's okay. I missed talking to you last night.*

> *Quinn: I think it'll be okay. I missed talking to you, too.*

Quinn could hear Sam moving around in the guest room while she dressed for the day. *I can't remember when I've been so angry. I don't like acting that way. It's not me.* She rapped on his door before she went down the stairs. "I'll make you some breakfast. We need to leave in half an hour."

Sam came into the kitchen a few minutes later and sat down at the table, where Quinn had placed toast with peanut butter, a cup of coffee, and two Tylenol. "I was obnoxious and out of line last night. I'm sorry."

Quinn looked at him for several seconds. "Yeah, you were. But I shouldn't have called you a drunk."

Sam chewed on a bite of toast. "The shoe fit last night." He sighed. "I need to get myself together."

The picture of Quinn and Caden was at the end of the table, joining them like a third person. Sam cocked his head toward it. "Can I ask you about that?"

"His sister lives in Hanover, and we've been seeing each other when he comes to visit her. We went hiking."

"Is that the real reason you broke it off with me?"

Quinn shook her head. "No. I didn't hear from Caden until after we were done."

Sam forced a rueful smile. "*You* were done. I'm not sure I was. Is it serious?"

"I'm falling in love with him." Quinn couldn't help but beam at the words. It felt good to say them out loud to someone.

His eyes sad, Sam nodded. "I really have lost you, haven't I?"

"I wasn't yours to lose, Sam."

"I know, I know. I'm happy for you. I didn't like the idea of you being alone." He finished his coffee before continuing. "I really miss you, though—not only the sex, but talking to you. That week in Boston felt like it was when we first met. I know you were right about me not being ready to move on. But could we stay in touch, maybe by text?"

Needing to stay busy, Quinn loaded the dishwasher. "I don't know, Sam."

"I know how needy this sounds, but the only other person I have to talk to is Jesse, and he's probably tired of listening to me whine."

She pulled her hair into a ponytail and looked at him with a mock grimace. "You think I want to listen to you? I can't be texting with you all the time." She remembered how often he had texted when they were together, both in their original relationship and after they came back from Boston.

He nodded. "I get it. But occasionally, if I need a friend to talk to?" He grinned. "I'll keep the whining to a minimum, I promise."

"Fine. But don't push it."

As they were driving back to the Sidecar, his phone dinged, and Sam swore softly after he looked at the text. "Son of a bitch."

Quinn asked him what was wrong.

"Norah just texted me. She wants to meet, misses me." He looked at Quinn. "Do you think this means there's a chance to work things out? Do I even want to do that?"

She shrugged. "That's on you." They arrived at his car, and as he left, she said, "Sam, I hope you find your answers. They aren't at the bottom of a beer bottle."

"I know. Thanks for rescuing me. I'll be in touch."

She drove away, berating herself for giving in. *Opening the door to communication? Probably not a good idea.* Her biggest fear was he'd go overboard texting her, especially when she was with Caden.

And she thought again about how she would have to tell Caden that Sam spent the night in her guest room. And the rest.

When she returned home that night, there was a package propped against her door. She picked it up and read the note. *I'm so sorry for my behavior last night. Thanks for being there for me.* Inside, she found a frame that matched the ones in her galley. She sighed and shook her head. *Oh Sam...*

Chapter Seventeen

I'm Your Girlfriend?

Caden

CADEN WAS LOOKING AT Quinn's picture on his phone. It was nearly ten thirty, and for the first time, he was nervous about making the call to her. He'd struggled to make it through the day, wondering who her friend was. She'd always been specific with him about who she was with, but her last two messages had been oddly cryptic.

He was working up the courage to call when Quinn Face Timed him. "Hey," she said, smiling. "Not talking to you last night made me miss you so much."

She was wearing the robe. Seeing her calmed his nerves, but stirred up other things. "I miss you too. Are you wearing anything under that?"

Her eyes sparkled as she grinned at him. "Nope."

His erection thickened. *Down, boy.* "Everything okay with your friend?"

"Yeah." Her grin faded, and his arousal vanished, replaced by the nerves he'd felt earlier. "I need to tell you something. The friend was Sam. He was at a bar in White River, and needed someone to talk to, so he called me. I drove over, and he'd had a lot to drink. I didn't feel right letting him drive, so I brought him home with me. He stayed in my guest room."

Caden had a visceral reaction to Sam's name. While Quinn spoke, his heart started beating wildly, his ears rang, and pictures from the bedroom at the Natick house began flashing in his mind.

When she finished and he was supposed to respond, the words didn't want to come out. "Wh-wh-what was his problem?"

Quinn's answer didn't register. He was sweating profusely and spinning out of control. *I have to get off this call.*

"Caden," Quinn's voice was faint. "Caden, are you okay? You look pale and sweaty."

He swallowed hard. "I... I grabbed a sandwich from the cafeteria, and it's not sitting well at all. I'm kinda nauseous. Let me call you back in a few minutes."

He hung up and put his head in his hands, taking several deep breaths. His heart slowed, and the pictures stopped flashing.

I knew it was Sam.

He hadn't expected her to be so open about it. *That has to mean something.* It must mean nothing happened between them, because if something had happened, she wouldn't have told him. She didn't have to tell him—he knew that. There was no way for him to find out.

He wasn't sure he was ready to talk, but he had to hear more from Quinn.

When she answered, he said, "I'm sorry, something didn't sit right."

"You need a good nurse to take care of you. I volunteer."

He winced. Quinn's voice was a combination of sexy and teasing, while Caden was struggling to keep his tone civil. "That would be nice." He cleared his throat. "I thought you didn't expect to speak to Sam for another ten years."

"I was hoping for that," she admitted.

"Really?"

"Yes." Her voice was firm. "He's in the past. There's nothing between us. But he was kind of a mess. He and his ex had been to mediation. He was drinking and needed a friend. And we were, at one time, best friends." She looked directly into his eyes. "I couldn't ignore that, Caden."

"He has an ex?"

"Didn't I tell you about that? How she moved out of their house while we were at the conference?"

"The only thing I remember you telling me about Sam was that he's not a part of your life." He paused. "I guess that's not true."

"You're angry." Quinn sounded sad. Resigned.

"Maybe a little. I'm bothered by my girlfriend's ex-boyfriend spending the night in her guest room." After a moment, he added, careful to keep his tone even, "Wouldn't you feel the same if an ex-girlfriend stayed with me?"

"I probably would," she murmured. "But I'd try to understand the situation, and I'd trust you if you told me it was an ex."

Caden read between the lines, knowing Quinn was saying he should trust her.

Before he could reply, though, she spoke again, and he heard tendrils of warmth in her words. "But wait. You're calling me your girlfriend?"

"Yes." *Too abrupt.* Softer, he added, "Do you mind?"

"Not at all. Caden, nothing happened."

"I believe you." He rubbed his temple. "I'm sorry. I'm not very enlightened, huh?"

Quinn said, "I understand your point. Is this our first fight?"

"Maybe." Caden sighed. "I don't want to fight with you."

"I don't like it."

Caden could hear the unhappiness there. "Me either."

"Are we going to be okay? Be able to get past it?"

"I think so. It means a lot that you volunteered it was Sam."

"I'm not trying to hide anything. I don't know why I didn't tell you last night." She paused. "Are you still coming up on Friday?"

"Absolutely. I just need a minute to process this."

"You really think of me as your girlfriend?" The teasing was back.

"Yes," he said, smiling a little. "How do you think of me?" He was feeling more in control, feeling that warmth he usually had when talking to Quinn.

"I've tried not to give you a label, but I like the idea of you as my boyfriend. Are you okay?"

"Yeah, my stomach's settled down. I'll talk to you tomorrow night." But just before he hung up, Caden asked, "Hey, did you wear the robe last night?"

"No, it was sweats all the way."

At least there's that.

Caden sat for several minutes, holding his phone and willing the uneasiness in his stomach to go away. He opened his phone and flipped through the photos from the weekend before, stopping on one of Quinn with the inflatables. Her smile was wide, and joy radiated from her eyes. His affection for her slowly replaced the tension he was feeling.

He found the selfie they'd taken with the colored fir trees in the background. His arm was over her shoulders, holding her close, and her head was snuggled in the crook of his neck. The aroma of her citrus perfume flooded his memory. She had pulled her beanie off just before he snapped the picture and wisps of her hair had tickled his nose.

I wasn't ever going to let myself feel like this for someone again. The depth of his feelings scared him. He walked to the bar and poured a shot of Irish whiskey, downed it, and poured another one. He sank into the couch in front of the fireplace, but he couldn't sit still. Taking the glass with him, he walked to the window.

The terror that had washed over him when he heard Sam's name came back to him. *What the hell was that? Not trusting her? I thought I was better than this.* He took a deep breath and downed the rest of the whiskey. *Okay, it's happened once. I need to talk to Quinn about it, and then it won't happen again.*

Caden dropped his bag at the guesthouse before going to visit with Claire and James. They had just sat down to eat, so he grabbed a beer and joined them. Rory cried just as he popped the top, but when Claire started to get up, Caden said, "Stay put and let me get him."

Caden walked to the front of the house, where Claire and James had set up a bassinet for Rory to sleep in during the day. He picked up the gently whimpering baby and cradled him against his chest. "Do you just want to be part of the action, or are you hungry?" Then Caden got a whiff. "Oh, now I know what the problem is."

He called out to Claire, "Do you have diapers down here? Oh, never mind, I see the changing table now." Hearing Claire get up, he told her to sit back down and enjoy her dinner. "I did a pediatric rotation. I can handle changing a diaper."

He returned with a clean Rory in his arms. Claire reached to take him, and Caden shook his head. "Finish your dinner. I can hold him and enjoy my beer at the same time."

"No Quinn tonight?" she asked.

"She's having dinner with some friends. They do it every year before Christmas. Then she's coming over to the guesthouse. So, you'll see a strange car in the drive."

Claire smiled. "Things are going well?"

He hesitated before answering. "Yes." He cooed at Rory, avoiding his sister's gaze.

"What's going on?"

Caden sighed and told them what had happened Wednesday night, filling in what he knew of Quinn's relationship with Sam. "Do you think I overreacted? Was I justified in feeling at least a little upset?"

Claire frowned. "How far have things progressed between you?"

"Wednesday night, I called myself her boyfriend. She seemed surprised."

Claire's eyebrows rose. "And that was the first time you've had that discussion?"

"More or less. Was I supposed to ask her to go steady?"

She snickered. "I think the kids today call it 'social-media official.'"

Caden groaned. "You know I don't waste my time on that."

Still laughing, she said, "I think grown-ups use the word *exclusive*. Not that I'd call you a grown-up."

"I'm as much a grown-up as you are," Caden said defiantly. He could see James shaking his head at their verbal sparring.

"Not the way you fumble around women." Claire shook her head.

"There's a reason I fumble."

Rory fussed, and Claire took him.

Caden rubbed his jaw. "I don't want to fumble this."

She gave him a sympathetic look. "You probably didn't have a right to be angry, Cade. She didn't hide it from you."

He knew Claire was right.

But Claire wasn't done. "She's not Mary, Cade. Are you still seeing a therapist?"

"Had an appointment yesterday." He sighed. "She called it a classic PTRS reaction. Post-traumatic relationship stress. A term I'd never heard before, but it fit. It causes panic attacks."

Claire nodded. "Did Quinn realize how strong your reaction was?"

"I'm not sure. She told me I looked pale and sweaty, and I tried to write it off as something I ate. Man, I'm a headcase, huh? I thought I was past this." He rubbed his temples.

"It's the first time you've let yourself care about someone. You're going to continue with therapy, aren't you?"

"Yeah. I was hoping I didn't need it anymore, but this shows me I do."

Caden visited with Claire and James for a few hours and walked back to the cottage at eight thirty. He changed into sweatpants and a long-sleeved T-shirt and opened one of the beers he had stashed in the refrigerator when he arrived. As the fridge door closed, Caden thought of something and went back to it.

The bottle of white wine he'd also brought from Boston was waiting there, and he found a corkscrew to open it. He dimmed the overhead light in the dining area and lit candles in the living room. He found a station playing the soft jazz they both liked and sent Quinn a text letting her know he was at the guesthouse.

She replied they were finishing dinner, and it'd be about half an hour until she arrived.

He smiled.

Chapter Eighteen

I Want To Make Love

Quinn

Quinn's dress for the dinner with her friends was red, shimmery, and sexy, accessorized with glittery earrings and a necklace. Instead of her usual boots, she wore black heels and said a small prayer of thanks there was no snow yet. She wanted to knock Caden's socks off when she saw him after dinner.

They had talked again on Thursday night, and everything seemed okay, but his reaction Wednesday night still disturbed her. And even though her heart fluttered every time she recalled him calling her his girlfriend, she knew what she had to do before they went any further.

But first, this would be Quinn's last time with most of the women before Christmas, so she focused on having fun with them. After dinner, they exchanged hugs and Merry Christmas greetings as they parted. Ashley hugged her and whispered in her ear, "Caden's going to be stunned by the sight of you. Have fun tonight!"

The drive to the guesthouse took Quinn through a neighborhood filled with large, old, beautifully maintained homes. This obviously upscale area was out of Quinn's comfort zone, and her nerves were on fire about seeing Caden. She hoped Ashley was right as she arrived at the address, turned into the drive, and saw what looked like an overgrown dollhouse at the back of the property.

Quinn knocked on the door, nervously tapping her toe as she waited for it to open. Caden answered, blinked at the sight of her, then blinked again. She grinned. She had on a black wool coat, had styled her hair, and was wearing more makeup than usual, which was a look he hadn't seen before.

"Wow," he said through a breath, "you are stunning!"

Smiling, she let him take off her coat. She turned around, and his reaction was exactly what Ashley had predicted.

"*Damn.*"

"You like?"

"I love! That is quite a dress." Caden finally put his arms around her, and Quinn melted against his body. He held her tightly, and she relished the feeling of his body against hers.

"Now that you've seen the full effect, these shoes have to come off."

He held her as she used her toes to ease the shoes off and let out a little moan.

"There's a reason I don't wear high heels very often," she lamented.

"The effect is as breathtaking without the shoes, and you know I can make those feet feel better." He grinned.

"I think you have a foot fetish," she teased.

He leered. "I didn't until the day we went hiking."

"Will you show me around this place? It looks like a dollhouse from the outside."

"It's small, just a living room, kitchen, and two bedrooms." As he led her through the rooms, he told her it was built in the early 1900s.

A vintage place was her dream, and she loved all the classic touches in the guesthouse. "It's lovely."

Caden poured her a glass of wine and led her to the couch, pulling her down beside him. But it was time, and she sat stiffly, not snuggling against him as she usually did. She had to tell him everything.

He cocked his head. "You okay?"

Quinn took his hand. "I know you're upset about me seeing Sam. I have some things I need to say, and I'm not sure where we'll be after that. But it's important to me to be honest with you." Pausing, she inhaled deeply. "I had sex with him in Boston."

She felt Caden's grip tighten on her hand as he drew in a sharp breath. *Keep going.*

"Afterward, we decided to see if we could rekindle what we had years ago. I saw him a few times right after we returned from Boston until I realized it was a mistake. He wasn't ready for another relationship, and more importantly, I didn't want to be with him. So, I ended it. Two days later, you texted me for the first time." She hesitated, taking a swallow of the wine before setting the glass on the coffee table.

"Nothing happened Tuesday night, even though Sam told me he's thought about our time in Boston every day and wanted to know if I'd done the same. I told him I hadn't, and that was the God's honest truth. Because ever since your first text, you have consumed my mind. I've thought about us not having sex, and for me, it's because when we do, I want it to be..."

"Making love." He finished the sentence for her.

"Yes." She looked into his eyes. "If knowing all this makes you not want to be with me, then say the word, and I'll leave. But I couldn't have a partial truth hanging out there." Her heart was beating out of her chest, and she struggled to control the trembling that threatened to overtake her as she waited for him to say something.

Caden's grip was so tight that her hand was going numb. But she felt his fingers loosen as he put his other hand on her cheek and said, "I don't want you going anywhere."

Quinn took a deep breath and blew it out before giving in to the shaking.

Caden drew her close, rubbing circles on her back. As he held her, he murmured, "You're okay. I've got you."

Thank God.

The trembling slowed, and Caden loosened his hold on her, pulling back to look at her. "Your honesty means more to me than you can imagine." He handed her the wineglass and took a swallow of his beer.

He sighed. "My reaction Wednesday night was stronger than it should have been, and I'm sorry. What you did before we were together doesn't matter. And what you did this week *shouldn't* matter, because neither of us has said we want this to be exclusive." He ran his fingers through his hair. "Hell, you weren't even thinking of yourself as my girlfriend. So, I'm saying it now." His eyes were very blue as he gazed into hers. "I don't want to be with anyone else, and I hope you feel the same way."

Unable to put words together just then, Quinn nodded.

"I need to tell you something, too." Caden took a deep breath. "I went through a devastating breakup three years ago that fucked me up badly. Going into all the details is definitely not what I want to do tonight, but I promise I will. You're the first person I've cared about since then, and apparently, I now have trust issues." He paused. "I've even considered if it's fair to keep seeing you."

Quinn gasped, but he continued, "My feelings are too strong to let you go, Quinn. I'm going to need you to be patient with me." He took a drink of his beer and put his hand back on her cheek, compelling her to look directly at him. "You're right. I don't want to just have sex with you. I want to make love to you." Her heart thumped.

"Quinn," he said, voice shaky, "I'm falling in love with you, and it scares the crap out of me, but it also makes me happier than I've been in a very long time." *That's the most sincere declaration of love I've ever had. Do I dare tell him how I feel?*

Heart swelling, Quinn put her hand over his. "Caden, I love you. The attraction has been there since I met you, and it's grown and grown. And I want to make love to you. There's nothing casual about this for me."

They abandoned their glasses and kissed deeply, desperately. Caden broke away first. "Let's take it slow. I want to savor every moment."

"I like that idea."

He moved Quinn so he could put her feet in his lap, and he started massaging them. "Is this good for a start?"

She moaned. "It's a great start. I don't know why I torture myself with high heels." For the first time that night, she let herself totally relax. His hands wandered up to her calves and then her thighs. Her dress was short, and eventually he reached her thong.

He pushed it aside and fingered her slit gently. Startled, Quinn gasped, and her hips rose against his hand. Caden leaned over, and their lips met. Her fingers twined in his curly hair, bringing him even closer to her.

His lips nudged hers apart, and he explored her mouth with an intensity she'd never felt before. Quinn felt it all the way to her toes as his finger slid against her. She squirmed with pleasure and plunged her tongue into his mouth, her fingers playing with his hair as his fingers explored.

They separated, and she grasped the hem of his T-shirt. He let her tug it off, and she said, a little breathless, "I've wondered what you'd look like shirtless." He had a sprinkling of curly black hair on his chest, and her fingers tunneled through it before moving down to his abs. "You don't get these just by playing ice hockey on the weekend."

He groaned, and Quinn enjoyed his reaction to her hands on his skin, knowing as he adjusted his hips, he was trying to make room for his growing erection.

Caden's hands ran up and down her dress, looking for an opening. "I love this, but it doesn't allow much access."

She stood with her back to him, inviting him to unzip the dress. He unhurriedly worked the zipper down, easing out one shoulder and then the other until the dress was on the floor.

Her bra was red brocade, and she was wearing a red thong. He growled and moved closer until her back was against him and cupped his hands over her breasts. His cock was hard against her back, and she flexed her hips, pushing against him.

Caden gently turned her around, and Quinn watched his eyes darken as he looked her up and down.

"You like this too?" she asked.

He nodded and moved closer, bringing her breasts against his chest. They both moaned, and his hands moved over her bare back.

"I want you," he breathed, scooping her up in his arms and moving toward the bedroom.

She giggled as he lowered her to the bed, and while he was still standing, she tugged on his sweatpants, sliding them off along with his boxers.

Looking him up and down as he had her, she let out a heavy breath. "Oh my..." His arms and legs were well muscled, and his abs, which she'd noticed before, were chiseled.

She reached for him, and he sat beside her before sinking to the mattress and pulling her on top. His hands rubbed her back and drifted toward her bottom, stroking as he moved his fingers closer and closer to the cleft in the middle. Her lips locked on his, and she relished the hardness of his erection against her.

Scrambling to a sitting position on top of him, she cupped her bra-covered breasts. He rose to reach them with his mouth, easing one out of the bra and flicking his tongue against the nipple. It hardened in response, and her legs tightened around him. His hands extended around her back and unhooked the bra, tossing it to the floor.

Caden sighed at the sight of her breasts and raised his mouth to one while his hand played with the other. *My God! I'm going to explode!* She continued to tighten and loosen her legs around him and rub her slit against his cock, unable to hold back.

Holding her tightly, he rolled onto his side, bringing her down beside him. He continued to suck on one nipple while he slid his hand between her legs, moving the thong aside to let him reach her folds. Two fingers slid easily into her wetness. They moved lazily in and out and against her clit.

Her heart pounded as she writhed against his hand, unable to stay still. "Caden, I'm close." Her voice was soft and sexy.

"That's okay, babe. Let it come. I'm getting so much pleasure watching you, feeling you."

He continued stroking her, intensifying his touch, and working her breast. The waves started, and at his urging, she didn't fight it. Her hips pushed against his hand, her breath quickened, and she let out a long, low, "Ohhhh, oh, oh," as the orgasm started. Her whole body trembled with it, and he held her until she quieted.

Wow! She rolled onto her back, took a deep breath, and let it out. Rolling back on to her side, she raised up on one elbow and smiled. "I'm not a screamer. My quietness is not a measure of how much I felt that. Thank you."

She leaned in to kiss him, and he sat up to slide the thong off. She quivered when his fingers touched her skin. "I still feel like I'm on fire," she murmured.

He removed the pins from her disheveled hair, and she shook it loose, her hair fanning out and over her bare breasts. The only things left from her party attire were the glitzy necklace and earrings.

Caden grinned. "You look incredibly sexy wearing only that necklace."

"You look incredibly sexy wearing nothing but that hard-on. We need to do something about that."

"I don't want to rush you."

"Rush away. I want to know if your cock is as amazing as your fingers."

Caden drew her close, her breasts against his chest and his shaft against her middle. Her hands glided up and down his back, drawing him even closer, before she moved between his legs to grasp his cock, making him draw in a sharp breath. She stroked the full length of him, and he took her breast in his mouth again. He moaned and thrust his hips against her palm. She smiled, continuing to stroke him.

He groaned. "Quinn..."

"I know." She let him move away, and he opened a condom, drawing it over his shaft. He held himself over her, lowering his head to kiss her as she ran her hands over his chest, moving them down to his erection again. She spread her legs, and he moved between them, pressing his cock against her as he slid his fingers into her again.

She was wet and hot, but she needed more. "Caden, please. I'm ready. I need you inside me."

He eased his way in, filling her completely. "This feels as good as I thought it would." Caden's voice was low and gravelly.

Quinn moved her hips against him and let out a deep sigh. He moved, slowly at first, then more quickly, the friction driving them both crazy. He stopped, and she knew he was trying to get himself under control. *Thank God.* She tried unsuccessfully to stay still, and as her hips rose against him, he nibbled on her neck, then started moving again.

"Is this enough for you?" He paused, panting. "Do you need more? My hand, your hand?"

"Not sure, but I'm enjoying this."

"I want you to get off, too."

She slid her hand between them, finding her clit. "You don't mind?"

"No, do what you need."

As he moved again, she pressed her clit against his cock, and the pressure was enough to start the waves coming for her. The change in her breathing made him pick up his pace. She came first with that same low moan, and Quinn felt his body shudder with his orgasm as he shouted her name.

After, they rolled onto their sides, both gasping for air and trembling. They clung to each other until their breathing returned to normal. Quinn sought Caden's mouth, kissing him thoroughly before they cuddled.

After the condom was dealt with, Caden climbed back into the bed and extended his arm across the pillow. Quinn snuggled close, laying her head on his shoulder. He sighed, a contented sound. "It's been a long time since I've shared my bed with anyone."

"I don't think I'm a blanket hog."

They both laughed.

She looked up at him. "You truly don't mind that I needed a little extra to get off?"

"I'm well acquainted with anatomy, and I know the missionary position doesn't always do it for the woman. My ego's not so inflated that I think I'm the only way. The important thing is we're both satisfied."

"Well, I know I am. Are you?"

"Satisfied and more. This was worth the wait." He punctuated his statement with a kiss.

She sighed. "I agree." After a moment, Quinn asked him if he'd been so considerate of his Tinder dates.

He snorted. "Are you kidding? Those were all about me. Which isn't me and is why I stopped, if that makes sense."

"It does. I've been with plenty of guys who didn't care whether I came."

"I care. I want it to be great for both of us."

Quinn grinned at him. "Is this a little weird? Talking about past sexual experiences when we've just…"

He shrugged. "Probably. I don't know why, but you are incredibly easy to talk to."

"I feel that too. Felt it the very first day at Harvard. I never chat with anyone like I did with you."

They drifted off to sleep, and Quinn woke up a couple hours later, still in Caden's arms but needing to pee. She eased herself out of the bed, glad there was a nightlight in the bathroom. His breathing had changed when she returned, signaling he was awake.

She wanted him again, just as much as earlier, and leaned over to kiss him. They met in the middle, apparently both having the same idea. This was an aggressive kiss, their tongues immediately dueling. His hands were all over her body, settling briefly on her breasts. Her hand went to his shaft as his mouth moved to her breast, wringing moans of pleasure from her. His fingers found her wet slit. Earlier it had been a leisurely exploration, but this was a fierce desire.

Quinn reached for a condom, tore it open, and sheathed his erection. He rolled onto his back, and she climbed on top, rubbing herself against him as his hips rose in response. She guided him into her, taking the entire length of him, and stopped for a second to savor the fullness of him before pumping her hips.

As they moved together, he sat up slightly, reaching her breasts with his mouth. His sucking hard on one nipple while pinching the other made Quinn moan and pick up her pace. His hips bucked against her. Breathing ragged, they both ground against each other, and Quinn suddenly arched her back, crying, "Oh, Caden, oh, oh, oh!" as she came.

His head tilted back, and he pulled her down onto him as he exploded. "Oh my God, Quinn!"

She collapsed on top of him and wasn't sure which one of them was trembling more.

Chapter Nineteen

Teaching Quinn To Skate

Quinn

QUINN WOKE UP TO sunlight and Caden holding two steaming mugs of coffee.

"I think I know your coffee order, but take a sip and see if it's right."

She pushed up to a sitting position, arranging the pillow behind her and bringing the covers up to her neck.

He grinned and handed her a mug. "Pretty sure I saw all of you last night."

"Instincts." She laughed. "It doesn't feel right to sit here with the boobs hanging out."

"Not a problem for me. Are you hungry? I can make you scrambled eggs and toast."

"Breakfast in bed?"

"Yeah."

She could get used to this. "Scrambled eggs sound good."

As he walked back to the kitchen, she admired him from behind. He was shirtless and had put his sweatpants back on. She thought about their encounter in the middle of the night and her center throbbed with the memory.

He returned with two plates of eggs and climbed into the bed next to her.

After a bite, she nodded. "You make a mean scrambled egg."

"There are a few things I'm good at." He grinned before continuing, "I assumed you weren't on birth control since you said you haven't dated in a couple of years, hence the condoms."

"No, I'm not. I had an IUD, but had it taken out when I moved here. I had some issues, and I hoped getting rid of it would clear them up. TMI for early morning?" She hesitated. "Sam and I used condoms. I've been tested for STIs, and I'm clean."

"I've been tested as well. And no, not TMI. I want to know everything about you. Did it help?"

She smiled. "Yes, everything is normal now."

"Would you consider something like that again? I'm afraid of getting carried away. It would have been easy to forgo a condom that second time last night. I wanted you so much."

She nodded. "Let me think about it. I'm not opposed. I just want to make an informed decision. But wait, I thought you Irish Catholics oppose birth control." She smirked and raised her eyebrows at him.

"This Irish Catholic is more opposed to unplanned babies."

"As is this druid."

He took her plate and mug, placed them on the floor, and ran his hands over her willing body. "Are all druids as sexy as you?"

"Not sure. Are all Irish Catholic boys as excellent lovers as you?"

He didn't answer, but showed her again how good he was.

Afterward, when they caught their breath, he asked her how she wanted to spend the day.

"I need a shower and, considering the only item of clothing I have here is my dress, I probably need to go home for some weekend-type clothes. Do you have any ideas?"

"If we were in Boston, I'd give you something to wear, but I have nothing extra here, so yeah, you will need to go home. I brought my skates. And I've researched rinks around here."

Quinn loved the sparkle in his eyes when he grinned at her. But... "I don't have skates."

"Found a place to rent them."

Pleased, she hugged him. "You thought of everything, huh? I've truly only skated at birthday parties many years ago as a kid. I'm going to suck."

He told her he'd take care of her, then suggested they could shower together. "It's an oversized shower. Should be room for both of us."

She thought for a minute before answering, "I'll shower with you if I can wash your hair."

"Do I get to wash yours?"

"Sure."

A moody botanical vibe dominated the bathroom. The wall behind the soaking tub featured flowers on a black background and the other walls were dark gray. The countertop was black granite flecked with gold and brass sconces provided the lighting. Ombre tile in the shower moved from dark emerald to the delicate green of the first leaves in spring and a window looked out at the forest. Boston ferns hung in the corners, bringing the outside in. Quinn took it all in and asked, "Did they make this just for us? It's beautiful."

While the water rained down, she washed Caden's hair first. "I love your hair. It's just the right amount of curly." She took a bar of soap and lathered up the rest of him. "God, you have a spectacular body. Those abs. And, oh, that erection. You might have a point about birth control. It would be nice not to have to think about that right now."

"It's okay," he murmured. "We can play." He rinsed off and started on her hair, massaging her head and working the shampoo through.

Quinn's eyes were closed tightly, trusting him as he guided her into the water to rinse. He soaped a washcloth and gently washed her back, butt, and arms before moving around to her front. He started with her breasts and then gently washed between her legs. She kept her eyes closed and sighed faintly at the ache he caused.

When his arms embraced her, they stood in the water, enjoying the feel of each other.

"We're going to be all pruney," she said.

"Or we're going to drown."

They both laughed as Caden turned off the water. Quinn wrapped her hair in a towel and dried him off with another one. He did the same for her, both savoring every moment.

She pinned her hair up and put her dress back on, making a face. "I don't know if I've ever done the walk of shame before."

"Don't worry about it. The only people who might see you are Claire or James, and they knew you were coming over. They'll be happy you spent the night."

They walked to the door and embraced before Caden slid her coat over her arms. He carefully worked the buttons, starting at the bottom. When he buttoned the last one, he gripped the lapels and looked into Quinn's eyes. "I really enjoyed last night. And this morning."

"So did I."

Caden grinned. "And there's more to come. I'll be right behind you on the way to your place."

At home, Quinn tried to do something with her hair and applied a bit of makeup. She put on a sweater, a puffer vest, and jeans. While waiting for Caden, she replayed every moment of the night before. The sex was everything she thought it would be and more—and it was better each time. She laughed to herself. *When was the last time I had four orgasms in less than twelve hours?*

Telling him about Sam was exactly the right decision. Having nothing to hide felt freeing. Finally, she thought about his admission about having trust issues. Eventually, he would share the details of his 'devastating breakup,' words that made her heart ache for him. She shook her head. *I hope he learns I'm a woman he can trust. The Sam admission was the first step.*

Caden arrived and asked her if they could stay at the guesthouse again, suggesting she bring clothes for the next day. "I want to introduce you to Claire and James."

She agreed, and after gathering what she needed, they headed to the skate-rental place and then to the outdoor rink.

Caden helped Quinn put on the skates and tightened them for her. She stood, wobbled, and promptly fell down. After picking her up, both laughing, he put his arm around her waist, and they started moving across the ice. Christmas carols played on the rink's sound system, and there were scads of other skaters, ranging from young children, some holding on to milk crates, to teenagers chasing each other around. Caden deftly guided them around the little kids and avoided the older ones.

They made several loops around the rink before he let her go, quickly moving in front to take her hands and skate backwards, pulling her along. After a few loops like that, he released her to gauge her steadiness, and she managed to stay standing. She grinned, and he moved beside her and took her hand, picking up the pace as they did some more loops.

He was full of praise. "See, you're doing great!"

She didn't respond, concentrating on staying upright. "Can we take a break?" She pointed to the benches at the side of the rink. As they sat down, she said, "I want to see you skate without me holding you back."

Caden took off on his own, went around a few times, graceful and quick, then skated backward over to her.

"Okay, I know nothing about skating, but you look pretty good."

He bowed. "I'm even better with a hockey stick in my hands."

She took a deep breath and told him she was ready for more. They skated for another hour, and by the time they were ready to leave, she was steady on the skates, able to move around the ice on her own.

While removing the skates, he rubbed her feet, and she whispered in his ear, "Better not do that. There are little kids around."

He grinned. "Later."

It was snowing big, fat, fluffy flakes as they returned the skates. They drove back to the guesthouse and had food delivered, pouring drinks, and sitting in the living room once it arrived.

Caden took her hand. "Let's talk about Christmas and New Year's. When are you working?"

"Christmas Eve until nine, and Christmas morning from nine to one. They make the shifts shorter to give everyone time to celebrate. Then I have the day after Christmas off and work the next five."

"I work Christmas Eve until three, have Christmas off, then work the next six." He thought rapidly. "Can we see each other on Christmas Eve after you get off work? I'll be driving up to have Christmas here with the family, but I'm probably going to head back to Boston on Christmas night since I have to work the next day."

"I'd like that, and it sounds like that will be our only time. Will you stay with me? I'd like to wake up with you on Christmas day."

"Yes, I'd like that too. New Year's Day is on Friday. Are you off? And the weekend?"

"Yes, and yes."

"Come to Boston. My fraternity puts on a dinner dance for New Year's Eve. It's been a few years since I've gone, and I'd like to take you. Introduce you to my friends." This all came out in a rush, and she smiled.

"What time does it start? I work until three, then I'll need to drive down. Will I be there in time?"

"They serve dinner at seven thirty with cocktails before, so there should be plenty of time. Is that a yes?"

She squeezed his hand. "It is. I'd love to go dancing with you."

He hugged her, and they kissed. "So, you'll stay the whole weekend?"

"Sounds like fun. Do you have other things planned?"

He nodded. "I've thought about a few things. One of my friends and his wife host a morning-after brunch on New Year's Day. We could go skating again, and the decorations will still be up in the city, so we can walk around looking at those. And I'd like you to meet my parents. If you're ready. Or... we can spend the whole time in bed."

"You present some very interesting alternatives." She laughed. "So yes, I'll stay the whole weekend. You need to give me some idea of what I need to bring for clothes. Are you sure about taking me to meet your parents?"

"I think so. My mom has been amazingly reserved." Caden shook his head as if in wonder. "She hasn't asked me one question about you."

"I'll confess, it makes me a little nervous."

His phone dinged with a message from James, inviting them to brunch the next day. He told her about it as they walked into the bedroom. "James said Rory sleeps in the morning. We'll get an hour uninterrupted to eat."

Quinn wondered if the new parents wouldn't want to nap if Rory was sleeping, and Caden assured her they wanted to meet her. He said his sister was becoming adjusted to the new normal and would welcome the company.

They sat on the bed, kissing until Caden pulled away. He grinned at her. "Do you want to take a bubble bath? I saw you eyeing that tub this morning."

"I'd love that." Quinn smiled. "It's not big enough for both of us, is it?"

"No, but that's okay...except can I watch?" The twinkle in her eyes gave Caden the answer he was hoping for, and he went to the bathroom to fill the tub.

Quinn removed her clothes and dug into the bag she'd brought to find her robe. She tied the sash loosely around her waist, and as she walked into the bathroom, she piled her hair into a messy bun.

Caden reached his arms out to her, and she nestled against him while the tub finished filling. He tugged on the sash of the robe and eased it off. He held Quinn's hand as she climbed into the tub, then watched as she sank into the bubbles.

"Wait a second." He walked to the linen cabinet and returned with a shell shaped pillow. "Now you can relax." Dragging a bench from the other side of the room, Caden sat down and gazed at Quinn as she reclined against the pillow with her eyes closed.

"This is heavenly." Her eyes opened, and she reached for his hand. "Thank you for suggesting it."

"Mmm." Caden sighed contentedly. "I could watch you all night. Did you like skating? I knew you'd catch on quickly since you ski."

"I did like it. Much more than at those birthday parties. I know you like the Red Sox, but do you cheer for the Bruins too?"

"Of course." He scoffed. "Is there any other team?"

"I have friends who like the Canadians."

Caden reacted like a dagger had been stabbed in his heart. "Nooooo."

Quinn laughed. "I knew that would get you. I've never been to a hockey game. Can we go to one?"

"Absolutely." They continued talking softly about things they could do together until Quinn started to shiver as the water cooled. Caden wrapped her in a fluffy, dark green towel, gently drying her. Then he held the robe out to her and reached up to remove the elastic holding her hair on top of her head. He nuzzled her neck as they walked back to the bedroom.

They made love much as they had the night before, with long, leisurely exploration as they both learned what the other liked. They fell asleep in each other's arms, and Caden woke Quinn up a few hours later with a kiss that turned passionate. Just as the night before, their desire mounted quickly, and they climaxed wordlessly together.

Chapter Twenty

A Flatlander Without Snow Tires

Quinn

THE NEXT DAY, QUINN woke up first, donned the robe and went to make coffee. She brought two cups into the bedroom, placed one on Caden's side of the bed, and climbed in beside him. As she sipped her coffee and watched him sleep, she thought about their most recent middle-of-the-night encounter—it had produced so much heat that just thinking about it was exciting her.

I've never been this horny for a guy... nor had this much sex in two days.

Caden roused slightly. His hand reached out to finger the satin of the robe, then his eyes popped open, and he rolled up onto one elbow. "I've been dreaming of seeing you in that again." He ran his hands over the satin and then underneath, brushing her breasts as his hand swept down her center.

Quinn wrapped her fingers around his erection and slowly stroked him. He groaned and fell back as her speed and pressure increased, his breath coming out in pants as he thrust against her hand. His cock swelled under her palm, and she was as turned on as he was when he came with a moan.

Looking at her with heavy-lidded eyes, he laughed. "You're still holding your coffee cup."

"I know," she said, smiling. "Don't move." Putting her coffee on the bedside table, she climbed out of bed. She returned with a warm washcloth and gently ran it over his torso. "That all happened kind of fast."

"You make me incredibly horny."

"I feel the same way. I've never climaxed this much, and all I can think of is wanting more."

"We can do that, although not right now."

"I know. We need to get ready. Can I tell you I'm nervous?"

"I understand, but you'll be fine. I think you'll like Claire and James, and they'll like you."

They showered, and Quinn asked if they should wash the sheets. Caden thought for a minute and then said, "No, I'm sure the housekeeper will take care of it."

She looked at him with surprise. "Housekeeper? God, I really am out of my league. I don't know anyone who has a house-keeper."

"Rest assured, we didn't grow up with housekeepers. Did I tell you the house belongs to Claire's in-laws? I think she worked for them and has stayed in the same position." He looked around. "You're right, though. Let's at least strip the sheets and put them in the washer. We did kind of mess them up," he chuckled.

Caden knocked lightly on the door of the main house before opening it. Claire and James were in the kitchen, and Claire immediately gave Quinn a big hug, telling her with a smile, "We're a family of huggers. Hope you don't mind."

Quinn didn't grow up in a hugging family, but she appreciated the warm welcome. "It's so nice to meet you."

"How was skating? Did he show off?" Claire looked at Caden.

"Um, I don't think so," Quinn said.

Claire laughed at her brother. "Don't let him dress you up in pads and make you defend the net against his shots."

Caden shook his head. "God, Claire, I was ten years old! You never let anything go."

James looked at Quinn, shrugging. "Get used to it. They'll go at each other like this all day." He motioned toward the food. "Fill your plates. We should have about an hour before Rory wakes up and wants to be held."

They sat down in the dining room to eat and chatted about the snow still coming down. Caden had told Quinn the day they met that Claire worked in the accounting department in the same hospital as she did, so Quinn asked about her job. They both lamented the newest budget restraints.

"I'm happy to have a few months off from thinking about that," Claire said, smiling.

When Rory stirred, Caden rose to get him. Claire told him to wait a few minutes, but he ignored her.

Claire rolled her eyes at Quinn. "He's very much a doting uncle."

Caden returned to the table with Rory cradled in his arms. Walking over to Quinn, he said, "Rory, this is Quinn. She's a special lady, which means you need to behave yourself. No peeing on her if the opportunity ever arises." He grinned at Quinn. "Quinn, this is Rory, the cutest baby ever born."

Quinn had finished eating and held out her arms to take him. His hair was as dark as Caden and Claire's, and he looked at

Quinn with big blue eyes. Holding him stirred a new longing in her, and she pictured having a baby with Caden. Then she chastised herself, remembering they'd only been dating a few weeks. But at least Rory was content in her arms, and she was happy to be holding him.

"Quinn's coming to Boston for New Year's," Caden said. "We'll go to the New Year's Eve party, and I'm thinking about introducing her to Mom and Dad. Has Ma said anything to you since I told her no questions?"

Claire's eyebrows rose in surprise. "We talked about what you said. I think she gets it." Looking at Quinn, she added, "Our mother isn't as bad as the picture we might be painting. She can be intrusive, but she'd also do anything for us. Right, Cade?"

He nodded.

They stayed until Rory cried to be nursed. Quinn reluctantly handed him to Claire, and they left to go back to her town house.

Caden's car swerved twice on the drive, and Quinn asked about his tires. He grinned sheepishly, telling her they were all-season radials. "In Boston, this much snow would be unusual. And I don't have to drive anywhere in the city."

She shook her head and affectionately muttered, "Flat-landers!"

He slid into the parking lot at the town house, and before entering, they made snow angels and built a small snowman. Chilled and covered in snow, they went inside, and Quinn brought out towels to dry their hair. For once, she hadn't had a chance to lay out a fire in the fireplace, so Caden put one together while Quinn went to the kitchen to make Irish coffee.

"I don't know if I should give you alcohol when you have to drive home," she called from the kitchen, and he replied he would stay long enough for it to wear off. Smiling, she returned to the living room, where the fire was already roaring. "Hey, nice job."

He nodded. "I was a Boy Scout. I've got skills!"

"Oh, I've seen your skills." She set the mugs on the coffee table and put her arms around him, pulling him with her to sit on the floor in front of the fire.

"You looked good holding Rory." Caden held her close. "Do you want kids?"

"Yes. I've always assumed kids would be in my future. I've even considered if I reach a certain age and there's no man in the picture, then I'll do it on my own. There are alternatives today to let that happen."

"Be easier with a partner, though."

"Absolutely." She sighed. "Single-mom life is challenging. I'd make sure I had a lot of support first." She looked at him. "I don't even need to ask if you want kids—you are enamored with that little boy."

"I am, and yes, I want kids. Not sure if I'd do it by myself, though. How many would you want?"

"I don't think I've ever assigned a number. But not five. I'm sure of that."

He laughed. "No, me neither. But I think more than a lonely only, as you called it. Christmas was fun with lots of us, but there was also a lot of fighting and drama. Of course, that might have been because four of us were female." He grinned at her, and she punched his arm before leaning against him.

He put his arms around her, murmuring, "This has been a great weekend. I truly am falling in love with you."

My heart. She took a breath. "I've already fallen. And as you said Friday night, it scares the crap out of me, but makes me very happy."

They looked out the window, where the snow was still coming down. Quinn picked up her phone to check the weather, which showed it continuing to snow until the next day. And the snow ranged all the way from south of Boston to the Canadian border. "You can't drive that car back to Boston tonight."

"I'll be fine."

She frowned. "No, you won't, not without snow tires." She considered the options. "This is probably crazy, but you could take my car and leave yours here for me."

He shook his head. "I can't do that."

"Because you're a macho man who can drive through anything, or because you don't want to let me drive your car?"

"Neither!"

"Well, then, why?" She would not budge on safety, and it was best he knew that. "Driving my car with four-wheel drive and snow tires—studded snow tires—makes sense. There's snow predicted for Thursday, too, so you'll have it for the drive back up here on Christmas Eve. Otherwise, you might get stuck there in Boston by yourself. On Christmas."

"You think I need studs?" He chuckled.

"I'm serious. You're going to be one of those cars upside down in the median."

Caden looked at the weather on his phone, then looked up road conditions. "You're really concerned? I honestly can't remember the last time I drove on snow."

Quinn heaved a deep sigh. "Yes, I really am."

His reluctance was obvious, but he accepted her suggestion, and they both agreed he should leave soon.

"One more thing," Quinn said. "Can I take your car to my garage and get winter tires put on?"

He stared at her. "Seriously?"

"Yes. If you're going to be driving up here, you need winter tires, or this will happen again." She put her hands on her hips. "I have a good garage I trust. I'd do it and surprise you, but I know better than to mess with a man's car."

"You can't pay for tires for my car!" Instead, he pulled out a credit card and told her to go ahead. "I can tell I won't win this argument."

She laughed, grateful he was taking her advice. "Nope."

"Are you getting me studs?" he asked, wiggling his eyebrows suggestively.

She rolled her eyes. "No, you're studly enough." As he put his coat on, she asked, "Do you have a snow brush?"

Caden shook his head with a sheepish grin. "I'll leave the one from your car, because I'll be in a garage once I get back to the city."

"That's okay, I have two." She dug one out of her closet and went out with him. They brushed off both cars, and Caden left, promising to call as soon as he was safely home.

Quinn tried to get things done around the town house, but anxiety kept creeping in. Normally, the trip would take about two hours, but it would be slower with the snow. As the hours ticked by, she wrapped Christmas gifts, did her laundry, and paced.

Finally, her phone dinged.

> *Caden: At the Hooksett rest area. I stopped to brush off the car and give my eyes a break from the driving snow. You were right, lots of cars in the median. Happy I have this trusty Subaru!*

> *Quinn: Halfway there! Glad you listened to me.*

Caden

The first thing Caden did at home was pour a shot, then down it, pour another one, and send Quinn a text.

> *Caden: Car's in the parking garage, and I'm at home. Need to make a couple of calls, answer the texts from Claire and my mother that blew up my phone, and then I'll call.*

He called Danny.

"Hey, Cade. What's up, man?"

"I just drove back from New Hampshire."

"Jesus, in this weather?"

"Yeah, I've spent the last three weekends up there."

"Ah, the nurse," Danny said sagely. "That explains why you've been MIA. No hockey and no Friday nights at O'Malley's. We were wondering what was up with you."

"It's new. I wanted to keep it private." He paused. "I need a couple of favors."

"Just say the word—you know that."

"Quinn is coming to Boston for New Year's Eve. I need tickets for the dinner dance."

Danny whistled. "That's a big step. It'll be nice to have you there again."

The second favor Caden asked for was a surprise for Quinn for Christmas.

Danny said he'd get back to him the next day, then asked, "Hey how'd your car do in the snow?"

"Actually, Quinn insisted I take her car. A Subaru with studded winter tires."

"No shit, and you left your car for her to drive?"

"Yeah. And she's taking it to her garage to have winter tires put on. I feel like she's taking care of me."

Danny laughed. "That's a change."

"Yeah, I kinda like it."

With that call out of the way, then calls to his mom and Claire to let them know he was home, he finally dialed Quinn's number. "Hey, beautiful."

"Hey, I am glad to hear your voice. I'm so relieved you are home."

"Me too. That was the most challenging drive I've ever done. Thank you for being pushy about the car. I'm not sure I would have made it otherwise. I can see why it's the unofficial car of Vermont."

"Do I have a limit to what I spend on tires?"

He chuckled. "Nope, after today I trust you to know what I need. Seriously, you made me feel very taken care of. It kept me going on the drive." A wave of affection swept over him. "I like it."

"I'd like to think we take care of each other." Her warm voice made him smile.

The last call Caden made Sunday night was to his colleague, who was working on New Year's Eve. They had discussed swapping shifts, which would give Caden the evening off, and that plan needed to be solidified.

First thing Monday morning, Caden changed the schedule.

His head nurse, Kim, noticed the change right away. "Hey, boss, someone messed with the schedule. It's showing you working during the day on New Year's Eve. That can't be right. Who's going to take care of the crazies if you aren't here?"

He smiled. Kim was one of the few coworkers he shared any of his personal life with, so he was pleased to confide in her. "It's true. I'm leaving the crazies to someone else. I'm planning to celebrate."

She looked at him over the top of her glasses, and Caden heard her unspoken question.

"Remember when I went to a conference at Harvard? I met a nurse from Dartmouth Hitchcock. We've been getting to know each other, and she's coming to Boston for New Year's Eve."

Kim gave him a hug. "It's about time!" She pulled back, then hugged him again as if to let him know how happy she was for him.

Caden went shopping at the end of his shift, then met Danny at the pub. They shared a couple of beers, and Danny handed him an envelope that would end up as a gift for both him and Quinn.

Chapter Twenty-One

Christmas Eve

Caden

CADEN DIDN'T LEAVE BOSTON until after six, hoping to arrive close to the time Quinn would get home. It was snowing but lightly, nothing compared to Sunday night. He couldn't wait to see Quinn again.

His desire for her was powerful enough that it surprised him, and he had qualms about overwhelming her, although they had definitely been on the same page over the weekend. He couldn't remember ever being so horny for a woman before.

The only other time would have been early in his long relationship with Mary, and he had been such a kid back then.

Immature and always stressed about her getting pregnant or their parents finding out they were having sex. And she had been very inexperienced.

Being older and in a new relationship definitely had some advantages. None of those things he'd worried about when he was twenty were even a factor with Quinn. Yeah, they both agreed they didn't want an unplanned pregnancy, but it wouldn't be the end of the world. He had even spent some time thinking about what it would be like to have children with her. *Too soon, of course. But...*

Those thoughts occupied his mind all the way to Hanover and made the drive go by quickly. He parked around nine and waited, patiently but impatiently, for Quinn to get home.

When Caden finally saw Quinn drive into the parking lot, his heart skipped a beat. He climbed out of her Subaru and called over to her, "Hey, that's a nice car."

"Thanks. It belongs to my boyfriend."

Caden grinned as he walked to the BMW. "He has fabulous taste in cars. And in women."

He took her tote bag and put his arm around her, then they made their way quickly to her door. Once inside, he put down the bags and reached to help her with her coat. She unzipped his jacket and tugged it off.

Caden's worries about overwhelming her seemed baseless. Her desire was clearly as strong as his. He put his arms around her and lowered his mouth to hers, and her lips hungrily parted, her tongue plunging into his mouth. Her hands traveled down his sides and snaked under his shirt, yanking it off only to find a T-shirt underneath.

He grinned and grasped the bottom of her scrub top to pull it over her head. His mouth sought her breast, moving her bra out of the way. She pulled on his T-shirt, and he tugged it off. Quinn flicked her tongue over his nipple while she unzipped his jeans. Her hand grasped his cock, which was already hard. He groaned and sucked harder on her nipple. Her hips thrust against him.

Picking her up, he headed to the stairs, pausing at the bottom. "Condom?"

"In my bedroom," she said breathlessly.

He climbed the stairs, stopping at the top, not knowing which room to go to.

"Left."

He entered the room on the left and placed her on the bed. She pushed his jeans to the floor and took him in her mouth while her hand stroked his balls.

"Oh my God, Quinn!" he moaned, watching his cock sliding in and out of her mouth.

She paused, and he gently pushed her down onto the bed, grabbed her scrub pants, shoved them off, and went back for her thong. His fingers grazed her folds, and she moaned as her hips jerked toward his hand. Kneeling on the bed, he lifted her up and unsnapped her bra.

He lay on the bed next to her, sucking on her breast and fingering her clit. "You are so wet."

She moaned and rubbed herself against him. "I've been thinking about this all day."

"Oh God, I was too. I was afraid it might be just me."

"Not just you."

Caden rolled away from her, trying to cool things off, but she wasn't having any of it. She reached for the box of condoms she had purchased on Monday. He helped her get it open, took one out, and rolled it over his shaft.

His hands moved back to her center as Quinn started stroking him again.

He gasped. "This won't take long."

"I won't need anything but your cock tonight. I'm close already."

He rolled on top of her, positioning his erection between her legs, and she thrust her hips up to take him deeply. He plunged in and out, the pleasure intense, until he could tell by Quinn's breathing that she was close. Her hips moved in rhythm with him, urging him to go faster. Then her low moan started. "Ohhh, Cade, I'm coming! Oh, oh, oh..."

The sound of her brought him to climax, and he groaned as the waves of sensation overtook him.

After a moment, he rolled off her, and they lay side by side on their backs. Once his breathing returned to normal, he murmured, "My God, Quinn, what you do to me."

"I think it's what we do to each other."

"Yeah, that's it." His stomach growled.

She giggled. "I have food downstairs."

"I don't think I can move."

"Me either."

After a few minutes, he said, "It's chilly. We need covers."

"Or clothes."

"Clothes? I don't even know where our clothes are."

"Scattered about from here to the first floor. It probably looks like a bomb went off."

"Probably."

A few more minutes went by, and Quinn said, "You aren't falling asleep, are you? Our time is limited. I don't want to fall asleep this early."

"Not falling asleep. Thinking. Savoring."

"Mmmm..."

"Hey, Quinn." He rolled toward her and pushed up on his elbow to look into her eyes. He hesitated. *I want to tell her how I feel.* "I..." He hesitated again and then leaned over to kiss her.

Quinn waited for whatever it was he wanted to say.

"I...I'm really glad to be here with you." *Shit.*

A smile blossomed on Quinn's face. *She has the sweetest smile. I love seeing it.*

"I'm really glad you're here, too."

"Everything about you is amazing. And I don't mean just the sex." He grinned as she laughed at his awkwardness. "Texting with you, watching you on skates, the way you are up for anything, the way you bullied me into taking your car and then took care of getting me winter tires. It's all great."

Her eyes gleamed, and she blinked as tears slid free at his words.

"Hey, hey, what's this?" He gently wiped them away. "I didn't expect tears."

"They're happy ones. I feel the same way. And it's far beyond the sex. It's everything about you."

Caden wrapped his arms around her, holding her tightly, until his stomach growled again. "Damn. I think I can move now, and I'm cold. You must be freezing."

"Do you have other clothes, or do we need to go on a scavenger hunt to retrieve what you had on?"

"I brought sweats. They're in my bag. I also have a couple of Christmas presents for you."

"I have a couple for you, too. Let me get dressed, and then we can go downstairs." She made her way to the closet, and it gave him a chance to admire her butt again.

"You have a great ass. It was the first thing I noticed about you."

Quinn laughed. "It was? I thought the first thing you noticed was the chai being knocked out of my hand."

"Nope, I saw you getting out of an Uber. You had your back to the building as you talked to Sam. You had on brown suede pants, and the way they clung to you gave me the start of a hard-on."

"Huh, and here I thought it was all about rescuing a damsel in distress when actually you just liked my butt." She came out of the closet dressed in sweats and warm socks and tossed a pair of the latter at him. "Let's go find something for you to wear with these."

Quinn

Quinn went to the kitchen to retrieve the charcuterie platter she had put together that morning while Caden lit the fire.

She called from the kitchen, "Drink? Wine, cider?"

He opted for cider, and she decided on that as well. The fire blazed, and two packages, as well as an envelope, were on the coffee table. She went to the tree, picked out three gifts, and handed him a long, awkwardly shaped one to unwrap first. He laughed when his unwrapping revealed a snow brush.

She giggled, too, and said, "I need my second one back, and I can't let you go back to Boston without one."

Caden handed her a rectangular package. She unwrapped it to find a book about the Appalachian Trail in New England. Quinn laughed and handed him a similarly shaped package, which was a book on hiking in the Upper Valley of New Hampshire.

At the same time, they both said, "Great minds think alike."

She handed him her last package, a hand-knit black beanie with a blue stripe that came with matching mittens. Grinning, he handed her his last package, which turned out to be a white cashmere scarf and mittens.

Quinn said, "I couldn't be out in the cold again with you in a baseball cap."

"And I saw that white cashmere and thought about how gorgeous it would look with your hair. I can't wait to see you on the ice wearing it."

"Oh God, how about just a walk in the woods?" She shook her head. "I'm kidding. I'm looking forward to skating on the Common with you next week."

Caden hugged her. "Good. I can't wait to have you out there." He handed her the envelope. "This is for both of us."

"Interesting." Quinn slowly opened the envelope. Looking inside, she gasped, put the envelope down, then looked at Caden with wide eyes. "What did you do?" Picking it up again, she took out the tickets inside. "You bought us tickets to a Patriots playoff game? That's too much!" But so close to perfect.

Caden smiled. "Don't freak out. One of my best friends works in the Patriots organization. I called him when I finished my trek through the snow on Sunday to ask about tickets to a playoff game. They're comped."

Now it was perfect. She threw her arms around him. "I've never even been to a regular-season game. *Thank you* seems inadequate. I can't wait!"

"Me either. It'll be fun. Danny and his wife are looking forward to meeting you."

Caden asked if they could go back to her bedroom.

She paused. "Let me tidy up down here so it's ready for my parents tomorrow. I don't want to face it in the morning before work."

"Let me do it after you leave," Caden urged. "I can let myself out. I don't want to waste any of our time tonight."

She loved that he wanted to help her. Still. "I can't let you do that."

"Yes, yes, you can, and I'll have it as neat as you would. Clothes retrieved, dishes done." He kissed her deeply, and she let him.

"Okay, but I am going to put the leftover fruit in the fridge." She stood, picked up the platter, and said, "I'll be right back." Quinn put the fruit away and paused before returning to the living room. *I thought he was going to tell me he loved me back there in the bedroom. He's holding back. I want to say it to him again. Hell, I want to tell the entire world.* She took a deep breath.

Chapter Twenty-Two

Christmas Day

Caden

THEY WENT BACK TO her bedroom and snuggled under the covers. He told her he had two questions.

"First. Why two snow brushes?"

"I keep one in the town house. Then, if it snows in the night, I'm ready to brush the car off without having to dig through the snow to get the one inside. It makes my life easier. I've developed a lot of routines you might find quirky, but they work for me."

"That makes sense. I won't make fun of whatever you do to make life easier." He blew out a breath, hoping this next one wasn't awkward. "Second question. Have you told your parents about me?"

"Not yet." She smiled reassuringly. "I will tomorrow. Although my mom probably knows I'm seeing someone, because her Spidey senses are strong."

"How would she know?"

"I haven't been texting as often. She'll pick up on that. I've talked to her but haven't told her much that I'm doing. She'll think that's strange." Quinn grinned. "*And* she will notice there's a new hiking picture and ask me who you are. That will be a good opening for me."

He had to ask. "Are you reluctant to tell them about us?"

"If I'm counting, that's four questions." She laughed and squeezed him. "Not reluctant, but in the past, as soon as I told Mom about someone I was dating, that was the death knell for it. It's been hard not to tell her about you right from the moment you started texting me."

"Are you concerned about it being the death knell for us?"

"Strangely, I'm not. Everything about this, you, us, feels completely different from any other relationship I've been in. I've told my mom before, in my late teens or early twenties, that I loved this or that guy, and she'd always push me on it. How did I know it was love? What does love mean to me? What did it feel like?"

Quinn fidgeted. "Obviously, she didn't like any of those guys and was trying to discourage me. Told me if I was truly in love I would know—it would be overwhelming, and I'd want to never be apart from the person I was in love with. Most of those relationships were long distance or definitely not full-time. Like one guy? For two years, I only saw him two nights a week, even though we were in the same town. But I insisted I loved him, and she didn't think I'd put up with so little if it was really love."

He gathered her closer. "And this, me, us? It's different?"

"So different. For the first time, I understand what she was saying. I'd be with you every minute, if that was possible. The feelings I have for you are like a giant bubble inside me, getting larger and larger. Overwhelming, but in a totally good way. I've never, never felt this before." She paused and looked deep into his eyes, then brought her lips to his.

Caden knew she wanted to say more. She'd told him she loved him that night in the guest house and he longed to hear it again. *But I can't get those words out and she's being cautious until I tell her how I feel. Doesn't want to scare me away.*

Her honesty struck deep inside him. He'd been in love before, and her description was right on. But then it turned out the foundation of that love was lies. *Don't go there.* He needed to share that with her, but not tonight. His heart had opened in ways he didn't think it could, and that was what he wanted to tell her.

"My feelings are overwhelming too, also in a good way. I think about you almost every minute of the day."

She grinned. "That might not be good for your patients."

"My focus is there when I need it, but most of the time, you're right there with me, too. And I appreciate your honesty. I'd like to meet your parents."

"I've been thinking about that. Their travel plans are usually fluid. If I ask them to stay an extra week or two, they'll do it." She smiled. "We could go up the weekend after New Year's. The football game won't be until the week after that, right?"

"Right."

"There's a hotel on the mountain. We can stay there."

"You don't want to stay with them?"

"No." Her eyes popped wide. "I'm not having sex with you in my parents' one-thousand-square-foot condo. And I know we're going to want to."

"You're quiet. We could probably get away with it." He waggled his eyebrows suggestively.

"Nope, not happening. The hotel is gorgeous, and we can go skiing while we're there."

He brightened at the thought. "I've only skied twice, so total beginner here."

"I won't take you on any black-diamond trails. Do you think you can get away for a long weekend sometime this winter? We could go to Florida and stay with them."

"Florida in the winter? Where do I sign up?" Then he thought of something. "If we're going to stay with them, we probably should get more practice being quiet. Because seeing you in shorts and swimsuits is going to make me want you even more, if that's possible." His hands began to explore her curves.

"The guest room is on the opposite side from the main bedroom, meaning it's not as big a deal. But yes, we should practice." She jumped as his hand cupped her breast, then she was kissing him.

Caden woke up at five to find Quinn still cradled in his arms, and her even breathing told him she was still asleep. He wanted to let her sleep, but wanted other things as well. This was the first time they had slept together and not awoken in the middle of the night to make love.

After a few minutes, she stirred and rolled toward him. She nibbled on his ear as her hand ran up and down his chest, eventually sliding down to his cock, which was ready and waiting.

She stroked him lazily for a minute and then said, "Do we have time?" Her voice sounded sleepy, but she was thrusting against him in the way he loved.

"We have time."

After their bout of morning sex, Caden rolled onto his side, gripping her tightly. "Merry Christmas."

"You're my favorite Christmas present ever."

"I feel the same way." After a few minutes, he suggested she shower while he made breakfast.

She laughed. "Are you wanting to watch my bare ass walk across the room again?"

"No," he protested, "I want you to get to work on time. But the bare ass will be a pleasant side benefit."

Once Quinn was in the bathroom, he pulled on his sweats and made his way downstairs. She'd been right. It looked a little like a bomb had gone off—her scrub top in one spot, both his shirts crumpled nearby. The gifts from the night before were on the coffee table, and he put on the beanie she had given him. It was comfortable, so he left it on, knowing she'd get a kick out of it.

He made toast and scrambled eggs, poured glasses of orange juice, and made them each a cup of coffee. Breakfast was waiting on the table when she came down dressed in Christmas scrubs.

Quinn clapped her hands when she saw him in the beanie. "I love it. Do you like it?"

"Yeah, I do," he said, grinning. "It's comfortable."

They finished breakfast, and he held her coat for her as she collected her things for the day. "I can't believe you made me breakfast *and* you're going to get my place ready for my parents. Thank you!"

He hugged her. "We take care of each other. Remember?"

"Yes. And call me when you get home tonight. Merry Christmas!"

He watched her leave, feeling happier than he had in years. *Best Christmas Eve in a long time. Maybe ever.*

Caden knocked before letting himself into Claire's house. The noise coming from the living room told him everyone was gathered there, and he hesitated before walking that way. He loved spending time with his family, but knew there would be questions about his absence the night before. Cathleen saw him first and leaped up to hug him.

"It's about time you got here." Her tone held mock anger until she added, "Although, it was nice having the guest house to myself last night."

Caden hadn't seen her in a year and his eyes landed on her hair, which was cropped short with the tips died light pink.

Cathleen grinned at him and ran her fingers through the fringe. "Like my new look?"

"I do. You look like a pixie."

Her knees bent in a mock curtsy, and Caden studied her outfit. While his other sisters had on leggings and Christmas sweaters, Cathleen was wearing olive green cargo pants and a simple white t-shirt. She was smaller than the other girls, and he remembered how ethereal she had been as a child.

Caden looked around at the rest of the family, finally locating Rory, nestled in Chrissy's arms and dressed in a red union suit with a tiny Santa hat on his head. He walked toward her with his arms outstretched. "Hand him over. You had all last night to hold him."

Claire piped in. "And whose choice was that?" She rose from her chair to give him a quick hug and whispered in his ear. "Did you have a good night?"

Caden snuggled the baby and nodded with a smile. "The best." He remained standing, content to coo at Rory while conversation swirled around him. When their mom got up and announced breakfast was ready, Caden handed Rory off to Claire and followed his mother into the kitchen.

Before she could do anything, he put his arms around her. "Merry Christmas Ma." They had talked on the phone but hadn't been face to face since Caden asked her to stay out of his business.

"Merry Christmas. Did you have an enjoyable Christmas Eve?"

"I did. The best in a long time." He helped her bring food to the table and when they finished, he said, "Thanks for giving me some space."

"I'm trainable." Mom smirked and then said, "We need to get everyone moving. I swear, getting all of you to the table is worse than herding cats."

Cathleen came into the kitchen with the drink orders and helped Caden make mimosas. "There's a new woman in your life, huh? Claire and James seem to like her."

"As do I." Caden grinned. "What's new with you?"

"I'm happy for you." She paused, appearing to give all her attention to putting straws in the glasses, then raised her eyes to meet his. "Not much. I'm thinking about coming back to New England. Have a job interview here this week. I'll stay in the guest house until New Year's Eve, then take the bus back to Boston."

Her news surprised Caden. Cathleen had left home for college and only returned for holidays. "I thought there was something holding you in North Carolina."

"Not anymore." Her eyes were sad, and she busied herself placing the glasses on a tray.

Caden hugged her and, knowing better than to pry, said only, "I'm sorry." He followed her to the dining room and sat between Chrissy and his mother.

When everyone was settled, his father raised his glass to give an Irish blessing.

The light of the Christmas star to you. The warmth of a home and hearth to you.

*The cheer and good will of friends to you. The
hope of a childlike heart to you.*

*The joy of a thousand angels to you. The love of
the Son and God's peace to you.*

This was the blessing that Caden's grandfather had said every Christmas until he died. Sean finished as his father always had. *"Nollaig shona dhuit."* He looked around the table. "Happy Christmas to you all."

They clinked glasses, and the stilled atmosphere gave way to mayhem as everyone spoke at once. When there was a break in the hubbub, James said, "Hey Cade, how did your car do in that snow last week? Claire was going crazy until you let her know you were home."

Caden felt his cheeks redden as everyone turned to look at him. "Quinn insisted I take her car. She has studded winter tires."

"Ooh, studs." Chrissy chimed in, and the entire table erupted in laughter.

When the laughter calmed down, his mother said, "Aren't you going to run into the same issue again if you keep coming up here?"

Caden sighed. "She took my car to her garage and had winter tires put on." He waited for more laughter, but the table was stunned into silence.

Finally, his father said, "Sounds like she might be a keeper."

Caden shrugged, then nodded with a smile.

After breakfast, they gathered around the Christmas tree, to exchange presents and Chloe said, "Hey Caden, do you want to see what Tim gave me for Christmas?" When he nodded, she held out her left hand. With a big smile on her face, she said, "I was waiting to see if you'd notice it, but you were too busy thinking about studded tires."

"Congratulations!" He leaned over to hug her. "When did this happen? And when's the big day?"

"Last night before he flew home to Wisconsin. We haven't discussed plans, but probably not until next fall or the following summer."

"That's great. Tim's a good guy." He looked at James. "And God knows we need more men around here."

James nodded in agreement.

Caden stayed longer than he had planned to, and as he got ready to leave, he said, "Hey Ma. Did Claire tell you that Quinn is coming to Boston for New Year's Eve? And staying for the weekend."

"She may have mentioned something."

Caden rolled his eyes at his sister as she flashed a guilty smile. "I'd like to introduce her to you all. How about if we come for dinner on Saturday night?"

The smile on his mother's face as she nodded told him he'd given her one of the best gifts of the day

Quinn

> *Caden: I'm home. Checking to see if your parents have left before I call.*

> *Quinn: They left around six. I'm home all alone.*

Her phone rang.

"Wish I was there to keep you company. How was your day?" His voice was the low and sexy tone she loved.

"Any day that starts with you making love to me, then cooking me breakfast can only be described as great."

"That goes without saying, but I was wondering more about the rest of your day."

She laughed. "Oh, that was good, too. The atmosphere on the ward is always different on the big holidays. We try to make the day special for the patients. There are a lot of visitors, a special holiday menu, and anything else we can do to make being in the hospital more bearable." She paused. "I imagine it's different from the ER on a holiday. It was a good shift."

"Anything else?" he asked.

Quinn knew what he was fishing for, but she wanted to tease him a little. "My parents were at the town house when I got there. It was good to see them. My dad grilled steaks, and my mom did the sides, so I've done no cooking at all today. We unwrapped presents, caught up on what's new in our lives, and played some card games."

"Quinn," he growled, "you know what I want to know."

"What? Oh, you want to know if I told them about you, right?" She grinned. "As I suspected, almost the first words out of my mother's mouth were a question about the new hiking picture. I told them almost everything about you—how you bought me the chai, how you started texting me, how you came to Hanover the last three weekends and last night. About the only thing I left out was what you told me about liking my ass. And what an incredible lover you are." She laughed. "They want to meet you."

"Your mom didn't discourage you?" She could hear the concern in his voice.

"The conversation didn't go there, and she knows I consider this something serious. She's happy for me." *Time to change the subject.* "How was your day?"

"Chaos. There's no other word for it. It's the first time all five of us have been together in quite some time." He was smiling now—she could tell. "We did lots of catching up. The big news is that Chloe is engaged. It was fun, but I was glad to head home.

I told my folks you are coming to the city for New Year's Eve and staying for the weekend." He chuckled. "I actually had to ask if we could come for dinner. Which made my mom ecstatic. We'll go there Saturday night. My sisters will probably be there too."

Quinn admitted she was nervous and reminded him he promised to tell her what she'd need to bring, clothes-wise.

Caden ticked off the list. "New Year's Eve, semiformal, wear the red dress. Brunch at Danny's and dinner at my folks will be informal. Bring some warm clothes because we'll spend some time outside. And don't forget the robe. Sunday, I'm taking you to brunch, not telling you where, but I promise you'll like it. Kind of dressy for that, like those brown suede pants."

Quinn was impressed. "Wow, that's very comprehensive. Most guys would say, 'Oh, whatever you want.' And I like how you slipped the robe in there."

"I want to see you walking around my place in that robe."

She laughed, then sighed. "I should let you go to sleep. You're getting up early tomorrow."

"I am. I can't wait for New Year's Eve."

The End

Epilogue

Caden

CADEN PUT HIS PHONE down. *I never thought I'd say those words again.* He sighed. *I should feel happier than I do.* The last twenty-four hours were everything he could have hoped for. Quinn's desire for him was as strong as his for her. He relived the way they had come together just inside the door, recalled pulling off her scrub top and the chill of her hands under his t-shirt, then the feel of her in his arms as he carried her up the stairs. His hips shifted to make room for his growing erection. *Down boy, six days to get through until we see her again.*

The family time was good too. There was the same good-natured razzing that went on every time he and his sisters were all together, but no one flounced off in anger. There had been plenty of that when they were kids. Cathleen was quiet, but that wasn't unusual. The sad look in her eyes when she admitted there wasn't anything holding her in North Carolina came back to him. *I need to talk to her.* He picked up his cell and tapped out a message.

> *Caden: How long are you staying in Boston after New Year's? Thought maybe we could have dinner while you're here.*

> *Cathleen: I'd like that. I'm staying until the tenth.*

> *Caden: Quinn will be here all weekend. Let's plan on Tuesday.*

> *Cathleen: That works. I'm looking forward to meeting her.*

> *Caden: She's amazing. Love you Cath.*

> *Cathleen: Love you too, big bro*

With time to talk to Cathleen privately set up, Caden's thoughts drifted back to the rest of the family. Rory had been a trooper, getting passed around, so everyone could cuddle him and never making a peep except when he wanted to nurse. That night at the bar, telling Danny he wanted kids, came back to him. That desire was an ache that ebbed and flowed but watching Claire and James with the baby had reinvigorated it stronger than ever. *Is that normal? I know women get baby fever and worry about their biological clock but...guys too?* He knew it was because he had fully expected to have his own children by this time.

As good as things were with Quinn, Caden couldn't forget that his life was supposed to have followed a different path. His gaze wandered around the den. *I didn't picture myself here, that's for sure.* He drummed his fingers on his thigh, then rose, walked to the bar and poured a shot. His eyes rested on a photo taken on that long ago trip to Ireland. His grandfather was on one side of him and his father on the other, with a castle in the background. Their smiles were wide, and Caden remembered the joy of that moment.

"Slainte Gramps." Caden raised his glass toward the photo. "Can you believe it? Me living in a place like this. We're all doing well, thanks to you." He took a swallow of the whiskey and then continued the conversation with his grandfather, something he did often.

"You've got a great grandson, he's a Brady all the way. Chloe's engaged and Chrissy's going to graduate high school this year. Something's bugging Cathleen, but I'm going to get to the bottom of that. Me? I'm great, met a woman. You'd like her. Yeah, even more than Mary. Do I love her? I do."

His glass was empty and he slammed it down on the bar. *So why can't I get those words out?* He stretched his arms upward and clenched his hands behind his head. *And why do I feel so melancholy?* He returned to the loveseat, stretching his legs out in front of him. The flames from the fireplace mesmerized him, and he remembered Quinn describing her feelings for him the night before. He had that same bubble of emotion growing inside that she did.

But I've felt this before. And look where it landed me. He shook his head. *I have to move past this.*

Caden climbed off the loveseat and strode to his bedroom. Opening the closet door, he reached up to the highest shelf and moved his hand toward the corner until it hit something solid. His fingers eased the object along the shelf until it was in front of him, and he could flip it into his hands. Catching it with ease, he returned to the den and set it on the coffee table.

Sitting down, he leaned forward to contemplate the box, with his chin propped on his left hand. Made of dark wood with a Celtic knot carved on the top, it was a little smaller than a shoebox. His other hand reached out and caressed the knot. Straightening, he reached for it and then drew back. *I need some alcohol for this.*

After refilling his glass and taking a swallow, Caden cautiously opened the box with his heart hammering in his chest. Bits of paper lay nestled underneath a baseball.

His mind went back in time to the day he left the house in Natick. His family, as well as Danny and Rob, had shown up to help him move, not realizing how little he planned to take. He had offered the furnishings to the buyer, and they had taken almost everything. The few things they didn't want, Caden had dragged, bit by bit, out to the curb every morning. When he came home at night, there was never anything left. He didn't want any reminders of his life there.

Claire and Cathleen were packing up his bedroom, knowing that he hadn't set foot in there since... Caden shook his head, took another swallow of whiskey, and remembered hearing the raised voices. He had walked to the bedroom and stood in the doorway, watching his sisters argue.

Claire had the chest in her hands and was about to dump the contents into a trash bag.

"Wait," Cathleen had said. "What if Cade wants something from that?"

"He won't." Claire's tone was decisive.

"You can't know that." Cathleen had become agitated.

The back and forth continued until Caden said, "Give it to me."

"But Cade," Claire had protested.

He had held out his hand and said again, "Give it to me." When she handed it to him, he'd taken it to his car, where he placed it in the trunk. It stayed there for the six months he spent with his parents. It was the last thing he moved into the brownstone, and he had shoved it into the farthest reaches of his closet without opening it.

Caden closed his eyes, then opened them and reached forward, resolute, his fingers extending around the baseball. The first Red Sox game he'd taken her to. They'd only been dating for a couple of months, and they'd had seats on the green monster in left field. A home run ball had come their way, the first and only one he'd ever caught. "You brought me luck!" He had punctuated his words with a kiss.

He rubbed the ball between his palms, savoring the leather and remembering the elation of that moment. The paper bag Caden had brought from the kitchen was on the floor and he dropped the ball in, enjoying the thud it made when it hit the floor.

Taking a deep breath, he pulled a handful of paper out of the box. He flipped through it, finding mostly ticket stubs. Bruins games, fraternity formals, a train ride they'd taken on Cape Cod and one to the Isabella Stewart Gardner Museum. That had been their first date. She was an art major and there was a special display she wanted to see. Museums weren't his thing, but he had happily trailed behind her as they explored every corner.

Everything was tossed into the bag.

Next, he picked up a poker chip from a trip they'd taken to Mohegan Sun Casino in Connecticut. They were celebrating her twenty-first birthday. Danny and Brooke had come, along with Robbie and whatever girl he'd been dating. Brooke had been the big winner that weekend, but that hadn't mattered to Caden. His grandfather had died months before, and he'd been happy to have the weekend away from the pervasive sadness that had overtaken his family.

Caden went through more ticket stubs, the program from his college graduation and one from his white coat ceremony. His breath caught when he picked up a photo. It was from the first fraternity formal they attended. She was wearing a black halter neck gown, and she'd left her blond hair swinging straight around her shoulders. Her blue eyes sparkled as she smiled at the camera.

Quinn couldn't look more different. His heart started pounding, and he took a deep breath, then ripped the picture in half. He exhaled and continued tearing the picture into increasingly smaller pieces. He held them over the bag and watched as they rained into it. His heart slowed, and he walked out to the kitchen for a glass of water.

God, I need to go to bed. He shook his head. *No. Not until I'm done.*

The box was nearly empty when Caden reached in for the last item. A three-caret diamond solitaire. He blew out the breath he'd been holding as he turned the ring in his fingers. *What the hell am I going to do with this?* The value of it meant nothing to him, but he couldn't throw it away. There had to be a way to turn the heartache it represented into something positive.

Caden rose from the couch and placed the chest in an empty spot on the bookshelves. It looked like it had always been there, and he was happy he'd be able to see it every day. Leaving the bag on the floor and the ring on the coffee table, he stumbled to bed, fully expecting to be awoken by the nightmare, but he slept soundly.

The next morning, Caden filled his backpack with clothes. He'd be working the medical van that evening and needed something warmer than his scrubs. Just before he left for the hospital, he made room for the bag holding the remnants of his former life. Only the engagement ring remained from the night before. Hesitantly, he picked it up, then jammed it into the side pocket of the backpack.

At the third and final stop of the night, twenty people stood huddled around a barrel, soaking up the meager amount of warmth the flames provided. Caden and Alan, a paramedic, climbed out of the van. As Caden strolled over to the barrel, he asked, "How's everybody doing tonight?" He found spending a few minutes talking casually with the group made them more likely to open up about any health concerns.

Marty, the unofficial mayor of the encampment, said, "What's in the boxes, Doc?"

Caden looked toward Alan, who was stacking boxes from the van. "Food, water, blankets. Stuff to make life a little easier."

"Oh yeah," Marty scoffed. "It's Christmas. Everyone makes themselves feel good by giving to the poor."

"There's room in the shelters. Your lives could be even better."

"Too many rules. You know that Doc. Harry's got a cough and Ned's got a cut on his arm that's looking kind of nasty."

"Let's get started then." Caden listened to Harry's chest, then gave him a shot of penicillin and a bottle of antibiotics. Looking at Marty, he said, "Make sure he takes all of those."

"Let's see the arm, Ned." Caden worked hard to keep his expression neutral when Ned pulled up his sleeve. "That's way beyond nasty." He looked from Ned to Marty, then back to Ned. "You really should go to the hospital."

"Nope, not happening." Ned growled. "You can clean it up, Doc."

Caden knew this would be the answer and took his time to do what he could with limited resources, while Alan checked out the rest of the people. Ned received a shot just as Harry had, and antibiotics. Turning to Marty again, Caden said, "He needs to get that checked in a couple of days. The van won't be this way again for at least a week. Can you convince him to visit the ED? I'll be there every day."

"Doubtful."

Shaking his head, Caden sighed. He knew Ned would never go to the hospital.

"We through here, Cade?" Alan asked, and when Caden nodded, he started putting their gear back in the van.

"Hey Marty," Caden called as Marty walked back toward the barrel. "Mind if I add some fuel to your fire?"

Marty shrugged. "Always grateful for anything you want to give us."

Caden grabbed his backpack and pulled out the paper bag. Crunching it as small as he could, he tossed it into the barrel and watched with satisfaction as sparks flew.

Alan was ready to leave, but Caden lingered. He reached into the backpack, retrieved the engagement ring, then placing his hand on Marty's arm, he said, "Come here." When they were several feet away from the group, Caden slipped the ring into Marty's hand. "Find a decent pawn shop. You should get a substantial amount of money for that."

Walking away, he looked back and said over his shoulder. "I'll stop by Monday night to check on Ned."

Afterword

Did you enjoy this book? If you did, leaving a review on Amazon or Goodreads is a wonderful way to let the author know. Reviews are one of the most powerful tools in an author's arsenal.

Sneak Peak

QUINN

They took a rideshare to the hotel, and once inside, Quinn followed the signs toward the ballroom, only for Caden to hang back.

"Quinn, wait up."

She turned to find him a few steps behind her, an odd expression on his face. She walked back, and he took her hand in his.

"Inevitably, someone tonight, after several drinks, is going to tell you how great it is to see me happy," he said, voice low. "My money's on one of the women, but hell, if might even be one of the guys. They've seen me at my worst. If they try to talk to you about it, can you tell them I haven't share all the details and you'd rather not talk about it until I do?" He ran his hand through his hair. "Christ! I don't know. I'm putting you in an awkward position."

This was a different side of Caden than the self-assured, handsome doctor Quinn had fallen in love with. He looked more vulnerable than she had ever seen him before, even the night she'd told him about Sam.

Quinn raised her hand to his cheek. "Caden, it'll be fine. Thanks for warning me. I don't want details about your life from anyone but you. I'll handle it. Let's go have fun."

CADEN

After several runs down the mountain, Caden went to the base lodge while Quinn did some tougher trails with her father. A wall of windows allowed him to see Quinn skiing, and he was impressed with her speed and grace. People started coming in for lunch, and a man with a young girl caught his eye. After a minute, he realized it was Sam. The girl must be his daughter.

Caden's heart began to race, he took several deep breaths to get himself under control. It had not crossed his mind they were in Sam's old stomping grounds too, and might run into him.

Caden watched them intently as they ordered lunch. Sam focused totally on his daughter, talking and laughing with her as they moved toward the counter. After they ordered, they walked into the dining area, searching unsuccessfully for an open table.

Caden took a deep breath and thought, *God, I'm probably going to regret this,* before he called, "Sam! Hey, Sam." As Sam turned to the sound of his voice, Caden waved, and Sam gave him a confused smile. "Caden Brady. We met in Boston. You're welcome to sit here.

Sam and the girl sat down, and Sam said, "I was not expecting to run into you here."

"Quinn and I are here visiting her parents. She and her dad are on the slopes. They should come in for lunch soon." Caden watched Sam intently. He wanted to be sure Sam understood he and Quinn were together—and he tried not to think about Sam sleeping with Quinn in Boston.

The story continues in Whispers of Starlight, coming on January 16, 2025

Quinn's Nutmeg Logs

1 Cup Soft Butter

  2 teaspoons Vanilla Extract

  2 teaspoons Rum Extract

  3/4 Cup Sugar

1 Egg

  3 Cups Flour

  1 teaspoon Nutmeg

  Frosting

Cream butter with flavorings, gradually beat in sugar. Blend in egg. Add sifted flour, nutmeg and salt. Mix well. Shape dough on sugared board into long rolls 1/2" in diameter. Cut in 3" lengths and put on greased cookie sheet. Bake at 350 degrees for 12 to 15 minutes. Cool. Frost cookie tops and sides, mark with fork tines to resemble bark. Sprinkle lightly with nutmeg.

FROSTING: Cream 1/3 cup butter with 1 teaspoon vanilla and 2 teaspoons rum flavoring. Blend in 2 cups sifted confectioner's sugar and 2 tablespoons light cream or milk. Beat until smooth and creamy.

This recipe was on a Christmas card my parents received from my newly married cousin Ann when I was very young. The cookies were a part of our Christmas baking every year after that and I still make them every year. Cooking tip? Call me a heretic but I don't sift.

Acknowledgements

Writing can be a solitary endeavor, but books don't get created in a vacuum. There are many people who contributed to Whispers of Mistletoe in one way or another. First, thank you to my early readers, Melinda Domings, Rebecca Maeve Hartwell of Hart Bound Editing and Deborah Ann Neary. Deborah gave me invaluable insight into big families and hospital life.

I also owe thanks to my daughter Katie who always answered my questions about how a twenty-nine year old woman might act. And for cheering me on.

The Sunday morning Breakfast Club, Steve, Candace, Eric, Bill and Margrethe, have continued to be a source of support, wrapped in gales of laughter.

My critique partners, Sally Walker and Sheryl Soffer. I've learned so much through our association and your insights were invaluable.

Thanks to my content editor, Rashida Breen and my line editor, Mary Morris, both from Red Adept Editing. I can't say enough good things about them. Their suggestions improved the story and my writing. I hope I'm able to work with them in the future.

Emily Hensley of Small Fry Marketing. Our association provided a much needed kick in the pants this summer and I can't wait to see where we go.

My husband Gordy has become much more involved in this process of the past few months and I'm thankful for his support and love.

And always, to my readers. I hope you enjoy following Quinn, Caden and Sam as much as I enjoy writing their story. There's a lot more to come.

Also by Sue Mills

Whispers of Goodbye

Whispers of Forgiveness

About the author

Sue is an avid reader who ventured into the writing world during the first year of the Pandemic. Her stories showcase men and women working to become whole and happy. Family plays a prominent role as do the steamy encounters which come with falling in love.

Sue is a lifelong Vermonter who counts books, sunsets, and travel as vital to her being. Mountains, from the slopes of Vermont's Green Mountains to the towering peaks of Colorado's Rockies feed her soul.

Her children are grown and flown and she's living her happily ever after with the boy she met in a college library fifty years ago.

Follow her on Facebook, Sue Mills – Author https://www.facebook.com/suemillsauthor

Or on her website, suemillsauthor.com https://www.suem
illsauthor.com/books/

Or on Instagram, suemillsauthor

And TikTok, Sue Mills, Author https://www.tiktok.com/
@suemillsauthor